One Night at Dornea Pines

Tifani Clark

One Night at Dornea Pines by Tifani Clark
© Tifani Clark 2015

Cover Photo via Deposit Photos: #126679204
Romance in Autumn in Park

ISBN-13: 978-0692529003
ISBN-10: 0692529004

An ABCD Publishing Book

http://www.tifaniclark.blogspot.com

Dedicated to my childhood
trick-or-treating partners.

Other books in the
Holiday Novella Collection

All is Merri and Bright (Christmas)
A Little Bit of Luck (St. Patrick's Day)
Losing Independence (4th of July)
A Heart Off Limits (Valentine's Day)
We Brake for Pie (Thanksgiving)

Other novels by Tifani Clark

Shadow of a Life
Haven Waiting
On Liberty's Watch

Table of Contents

One Night at Dornea Pines

Tifani Clark

Chapter 1

Samantha Alwood struggled to balance her purse, a water bottle, and a stack of folders as she attempted to open the door to her office. She also held a chocolate pastry between her teeth and her cell phone to her ear. Every time she managed to get a grip on the doorknob, the stack of folders would start to slip. The more she tried, the more frustrated she became. With a defeated growl, she kicked at the door with her red high heel, hoping one of her two assistants would hear the muffled thumps and come to her rescue.

The door opened a moment later to reveal a smiling Destiny. "Sam? What are you doing?"

Samantha stormed past her and dropped the pile of folders on the nearest chair. Removing the pastry from her mouth, she snapped, "I'm trying to get in. What else would I be doing?"

Destiny's lips turned down and she shook her head. "Judging by your oh-so-happy demeanor, I'm going to take a wild stab in the dark and guess that you didn't win the auction this morning."

Samantha plopped into the chair next to the one where she'd dropped the folders and took a bite of her pastry. "I'm sorry. The auction was so frustrating I've been seething ever since I left. I didn't mean to take it out on you."

Destiny put her hands on her hips. "I don't get it. We researched that property forever. There is no way your bid wasn't competitive."

"Our bid wasn't even close."

"Who could possibly afford to pay more than we were offering and still make money flipping that place?"

Samantha took another bite of the pastry and a glob of strawberry jelly oozed out and dropped onto her navy skirt. Completely defeated, she didn't even bother to wipe it up. "I'll give you exactly one guess."

"Kyle Shipton," Megan called from her cluttered desk across the room.

Samantha stopped staring at the red blob and raised her eyes to her assistant. "That's the one."

"Grr." Destiny slapped a hand on her desk. "He's the most frustrating person in this business. How does he keep beating us out?"

"The only thing I can figure," Samantha began, "is that he's got a lot of money already and this is just a hobby. If this were his only means of support for himself and his family, I don't think he'd still be in business."

"Kyle has a family?" Megan asked. "I thought he was the spawn of the devil. I'm surprised he found someone that would show interest in him."

"I know nothing about the guy's personal life. All I

know is that he keeps beating us out at auctions. If this keeps up, we'll all be looking for new jobs. Maybe he's married and maybe he's not. For all I know, he lives in his parents' basement." Samantha looked at Destiny with raised eyebrows.

Destiny raised her shoulders and dropped them again. "Don't look at me. I've only met the guy one time. It was a few months ago when I went to an auction with you."

Samantha sighed and stood up. The glob of jelly she'd been ignoring rolled off her skirt and onto the floor. She snatched a tissue off Megan's desk and wiped it up. "It doesn't matter. What matters is that we don't let him beat us again. He's starting to make a habit of this and I'm getting tired of it. Got it?"

"Yes, Ma'am." Megan put one hand to her forehead and saluted her boss.

Samantha rolled her eyes, but grinned anyway. "That pastry didn't quite ease my frustration. I'll be in my office, raiding the chocolate stash in my bottom drawer." She straightened the pile of folders on the chair next to her before picking them up and tucking them under her arm.

Alone in her office, Samantha dropped into her chair and swiveled around to look out her window. From her fourth story office, she had an unimpeded view of the mountains along the east side of Provo. She'd spent countless hours hiking the trails scattered across those mountains. During her teen years, her father would run the trail along the Provo River with her every morning before she left for school.

Spending time with her father meant a lot to her, but living up to his success was even more important. Her father ran his own real estate agency for forty years before turning his contact list over to Samantha and taking early retirement. Her parents had been traveling the country in their motor home for two years, sending postcards from whatever destination caught their current whim.

As a teenager and then while completing her business degree at Utah Valley University, Samantha worked for her father. She knew the ins and outs of the business and wanted nothing more than for her own company to be just as competitive. Unlike her father, she'd chosen to put all her focus on flipping houses. She hired Destiny and Megan to work with her. Megan followed leads and did most of the research on a property and Destiny put the final touches on the homes before selling them. Managing everyone and overseeing the remodels fell to Samantha.

Watching a home nobody wanted anymore come to life again felt magical to her. She didn't, however, enjoy going to auction after auction only to be outbid by Kyle Shipton.

Samantha didn't lie when she told her assistants she knew nothing about his personal life. They talked to each other at every foreclosure auction, but those words usually consisted of playful banter and jabs at each other. Try as she might, she couldn't think of a single time when Kyle didn't have a wide grin plastered on his face. She never quite knew if it was part of his personality or his way of mocking her and the other bidders. *He must be married. No man could dress that nice without a woman influencing his choices. And his hair is always perfectly combed. And the way he smells...*

Samantha shook herself from her thoughts, refusing to give any more thought to her nemesis. She swiveled her chair away from the window and began the daily task of listening to her messages and returning what sometimes felt like an endless list of phone calls. "The appliances absolutely have to be in by Friday," she said into the phone while speaking to one of her contractors. "Waiting until next week is completely unacceptable. The open house for that property is already set for Monday. I'm not changing it."

Samantha's door opened and Megan stepped in. She held up a finger, motioning for her assistant to give her a minute.

"I've got someone waiting to meet with me, Hardy, so I'll have to go. I'll be over Friday evening to see the new appliances. I'm sure they will look great and be completely ready to go. Goodbye." She hung up the phone without waiting for a response.

"Sorry," Megan said. "I didn't mean to interrupt."

"Actually, that was great timing. He's trying to back out of the dates we agreed upon for the property over on Butterfly Drive. Your entrance gave me a way to get off the phone. What's up?"

Megan tucked one of her red curls behind her ear and handed a sheet of paper to Samantha. "It's a list of the newest potential properties to buy."

"More auctions?" Samantha asked as she set the paper on the desk in front of her.

Megan shook her head. "Not this time. All of these homes are being sold by the owners. Some have posted pictures online and most of the prices seem reasonable for the condition they're in. You'd have to check them out, of course. One of the houses has two big floors plus an attic, five bedrooms, and three bathrooms. *And,* the best part of all, it sits on three acres. *Three!* That's unheard of at the price they're asking."

"You're sure it's not out of our price range?"

Megan nodded. "Unless the ad was a typo, it's very much doable."

Samantha held the memo up. "Which one is it?"

Megan pointed to an item on the list.

"114 Dornea Avenue," Samantha whispered. "Why does that address sound so familiar?"

Megan shrugged. "Don't ask me. I've only lived in this area for a year and a half. Remember?"

Samantha rolled across the wood floor in her chair and stared at the map of Provo on the back wall of her office. Suddenly she jumped out of her chair. "Oh my gosh! I think I know where this is!"

"And...it's a good thing?"

"It's a *really* good thing."

"Care to expand on that?"

"We can talk while we're driving."

Megan raised her eyebrows. "To the house? You want me to come?"

Samantha grabbed her purse off her desk and made sure her car keys were inside before turning back to Megan. "I'll definitely need a second opinion on this, but if it's the home I'm thinking of, and the owner really only wants the price you wrote down, we could make a killing on this project. This could be our crowning moment."

"Should I get Destiny, too?"

Samantha shook her head. "Someone needs to stay here and answer the phones. Besides, I know Destiny and she won't like this excursion."

"Why not?"

"Because. We're going to visit a *very* haunted house."

Samantha couldn't help but feel anxious as she drove through town in her two-door silver car. Next to her, Megan took the time to file her nails and reapply her lipstick.

"Care to explain what you meant about the house being haunted?" she asked Samantha.

"When I was a child growing up here, there was a big old house on Dornea Avenue. Usually it sat vacant, but there were a few times when someone actually lived there. They'd start cleaning up the place, fixing fences, trimming trees, and then the repairs would suddenly stop and it would sit vacant again. Rumors about that place being haunted have been circulating since long before I was born. Supposedly everyone that has ever tried to live there gets chased away by ghosts."

"That's sounds creepy. Do you believe in that kind of stuff?"

Samantha laughed. "Absolutely not, but that's why I know this place is going to be a steal. People in this town and area are so scared of it, they'll stay away. We'll get it for dirt cheap, change it so it's not even recognizable, and flip it for a huge profit. What about you? Do you believe in ghosts?"

Megan sighed. "No. At least, I think I don't. I've never experienced anything that would make me believe. Maybe I'd change my mind if something weird happened."

"True."

"What are the rumors? What makes people think it's haunted?" Megan asked.

"The story changes depending on who's telling it. The most common version claims that the wife of the original owner haunts it. Her husband was killed in World War I and she still paces the house, waiting for him to come home. There are a lot of trees on the property and people say they've seen her floating through there."

"Sounds kind of disturbing," Megan said with a smile.

"I know, right? Another version I've heard is similar, but it's a woman looking for a lost child. She walks, or floats, or flies, or whatever it is ghosts do while calling out her son's name. Others insist they've seen the ghost of the little boy she's looking for, but the two ghosts can't seem to find each other.

"That's a sad story."

"I'm sure it's not true. It sounds like every other haunted house story out there. And I don't know if it's accurate or not, but supposedly there's an old graveyard on the property."

Megan pulled her jacket tighter. "A haunted house and an old graveyard—are you sure you're not just trying to get me in the mood for Halloween in a couple of days?"

"Positive." Samantha smiled. "Of course, the fact that Halloween is close might make interest in the property rise. The timing could be bad for us."

"You sound like you know a lot about the place. Have you actually been inside?"

Samantha shook her head. "Never. I don't know

anyone that ever has."

"So for all we know, the kitchen could be painted purple with yellow polka dots?"

"Exactly." Samantha laughed. "I did see the exterior once. The house is set so far back from the road, and there're so many trees, you can't see it just by driving by. Kids were constantly daring each other to try to get inside the gates...especially around Halloween."

"Is that how *you* saw the outside?"

Samantha turned her car onto narrow Dornea Avenue and glanced at Megan in the passenger seat. "Perhaps." She winked. "A couple of friends and I crawled under the gate once and walked up the lane. We planned to take pictures on the porch to prove we'd been there, but about the time the home came into view, a light turned on in an upstairs window. We didn't want to get in trouble for trespassing so we got out of there pretty fast."

"Was someone home...or was it the *ghost*?" Megan said in a spooky voice.

"Nice try. I saw a moving truck go through the gates the next day. I doubt it had anything to do with supernatural beings."

"Still, you never know."

The road wound up the hillside, passing only a few homes tucked amongst the trees. Leaves of all colors covered the surface of the road in a sea of reds, oranges, and yellows. The leaves churned and swirled as Samantha's tires stirred them up. A moment later, she pulled to the shoulder of the road. A tiny portion of the home she remembered from her youth could still be seen through the trees.

Megan leaned forward in her seat and peered out

the passenger side window. "I see why everyone dared each other to go inside. It definitely gives off a haunted house vibe." She tucked another red curl behind her ear. "You were right not to bring Destiny. Her imagination would be coming up with all kinds of crazy scenarios right about now."

"See. I know what I'm doing sometimes." Samantha grabbed her purse off the back seat where she'd tossed it and climbed out of the car. A cold autumn breeze swirled her brown her around her face. She pulled a rubber band off her wrist and pulled her hair back in a loose ponytail before zipping her jacket up to her chin. Her red heels crunched through the dead and decaying leaves as she approached the closed gates leading to the home.

A rock fence at least eight feet high surrounded the entire property, impeding their view. An iron gate blocked the only access to the property and it was held closed by a heavy padlock.

Samantha turned at the sound of Megan's arrival next to her. "What do you think?"

Megan reached forward and rattled the lock. "I think maybe we should have called before driving over here, Sam."

"No way. I didn't want the owner tipped off that I know the history of the property. I wasn't positive just by knowing the address so I had to make sure it was really Dornea Pines for sale."

Megan stuck her nose through the slats of the iron gates. "We can only see a corner of the house from here. What if the entire back half of it has collapsed in on itself? And what's with all the pine trees? I didn't know those grew around here."

Samantha pointed at the gate where the words

Dornea Pines were formed in an arc of the metal slats. "Do you really need to ask that last question?" she said with a smile.

"Good point."

Samantha reached into her purse and pulled out her cell phone. "I'm sure the owner will give us a tour if we call. For the price you said they're asking we could knock down the house and just sell the empty acreage. We'd still make a profit. I'm starting to think that the condition of the home is irrelevant."

Megan frowned and turned to Samantha. "There has to be a catch. Now that I've seen where the place is, I'm more convinced the price in the ad was a typo."

"You're probably right, but if it is real, I'll be kicking myself forever if we don't at least check it out." She tapped the buttons on her phone. "Read me the last four digits of the phone number. I can't see them from this angle."

Megan moved over a few paces and peered at the *For Sale by Owner* sign on the other side of the gate. "7831," she answered.

"Thanks." Samantha drummed her fingers on the fence while she waited for someone to answer on the other end of the line.

"*Hello?*" A male voice answered

"Hi. This is Samantha Alwood. I'm calling in reference to the home listed for sale at 114 Dornea Avenue in Provo."

"*I'm overseeing the sale on behalf of the owner. How may I help you?*"

"I'd like to set up a time to come and look at the home. Today would be ideal, but I could make tomorrow work."

"*I'm afraid that isn't possible.*"

Samantha glanced at Megan. She really hoped the property hadn't sold in the few hours since it had been listed. "I'd really like to see more of the property than I can see from the closed gate. I could try to move things around on my schedule to find a time that is more convenient for you. Is there a day or time that would work better for *your* schedule?"

The man on the phone cleared his throat and then paused before responding. *"I'm sorry, but the owner has given strict instructions that absolutely no one be allowed on the property. No exceptions."*

Chapter 2

Those were not the words Samantha expected to hear. Shocked, her mouth struggled to form words and it took her a moment to respond. "Sir, if no one is allowed to look at the home, how does the owner expect to sell it?"

Hearing Samantha's half of the conversation, Megan looked up with raised eyebrows. "We can't see it?" she whispered.

Samantha waved her away with her hand.

"*I understand that it might turn some buyers off, but those are the rules of the sale. The home and property are fairly priced for the circumstances. All the furnishings currently in the home are also included in the price. If you'd like to submit an offer, you may email me at the address listed in the advertisement. Is there anything else I can help you with?*"

"Yes. Have there been any offers yet?"

"*Not yet. The ad was only posted a couple of hours*

ago."

"I see. Thank you for your time." Samantha turned off her phone and stomped toward her car. "This is completely ridiculous."

Megan hurried to catch up. "What's going on?"

"They're not letting anyone past the gates. Anyone who buys the home has to do it sight unseen."

"That's crazy!"

"My thoughts exactly."

"What are you going to do?"

Samantha drummed her fingers on the roof of the car. "I'm not sure yet."

"If you ask me, it sounds like they're hiding something."

"It does seem fishy." Samantha chewed on her lip. "Or it could just mean that someone still lives there and doesn't like the idea of strangers traipsing through their home."

"I guess it could be something like that, but it feels like a scam to me."

The two women climbed into Samantha's car and she turned the key in the ignition. Just as the car came to life, another vehicle came up the road. The blue sedan slowed as it neared them and then stopped completely in front of the gates. The windows were tinted so the driver couldn't' be seen. After a few moments, the car took off and continued farther up Dornea Avenue.

"Competition or creep?" Megan asked.

"Hopefully neither," Samantha answered.

The pair drove back to the office in silence, both lost in their own thoughts. Samantha had seen Dornea Pines as a teen. She *had* to have that house. In her mind, she could already see it restored to what she imagined as its former beauty.

Destiny glanced up from her computer screen when the women entered the office a short time later. "How'd it go? Did the property look alright?"

Samantha nodded to Megan. "You explain. I'll be in my office crunching numbers."

"Want some help?" Megan asked.

"Sure. Since we can't see the house, we'll have to operate on the idea that we'll tear the house down and sell just the property. If we can salvage the house, it will be a bonus. You do some math and I'll do some math and if we're even close, we'll go for it."

Megan hurried to her desk. "I'll get right on it."

"Right after she explains to me what's going on," Destiny called just before Samantha closed her door.

In her office, Samantha tossed her purse onto a chair and hurried to sit down at her desk. She tapped her fingers on her desk while waiting for her computer to wake up. Her mind and thoughts were in a million different places as she clicked the icon to pull up her favorite search engine. She made a site detailing some of Provo's historic homes and neighborhoods her first stop. She'd used the site more than once in the past when considering different properties to flip.

"What secrets can you tell me about Dornea Pines?" she whispered as she clicked on different home images. She spent the next hour hunting, but even though photos of Dornea Pines looking like a haunted house littered social media, she couldn't find a single photograph of the home in its original state. If she'd wanted a photo of teens standing in front of the home or just outside the gates, it would have been her lucky day because she hit the jackpot. Unfortunately, all the pictures were taken in the dark so even the most recent ones didn't reveal the condition of the home.

Abandoning her mission, she went to work figuring costs instead. Since none of the few homes on Dornea Avenue had changed hands in the past five years, she had to base her numbers on nearby streets and similar-sized lots. She added and subtracted, while chewing on her eraser and multiplied and divided, while tapping her foot on the ground. She'd never felt that much anxiety over buying a property before. But, no matter how she figured the numbers, buying Dornea Pines seemed like the deal of the century.

Samantha hit the intercom button on her phone. "Megan, Destiny, get in here."

Seconds later, both women entered. "Are you ready for my opinion?" Megan asked.

Samantha shifted in her chair. "I've got an idea of what we'll have to spend and what we can sell it for. We'll exchange offer prices on the count of three. Deal?"

Megan nodded. "One...two...three."

Each woman traded papers with the other. Smiles spread across both their faces.

"Somebody better tell me what the result is," Destiny said. "You're both being so vague today. It's annoying."

Samantha continued to grin. "Our cost interpretations are almost identical. Both numbers prove we should move forward on this house." She leaned back in her chair and crossed her arms over her chest. "After losing this morning's auction, I thought my weekend was ruined. I think it just turned around. Now, get out of here so I can make an offer."

Samantha returned to her computer and quickly typed an email stating her official offer. Even though the owner's asking price was more than fair, she came in just under the asking price. She needed wiggle room if—when—the owner decided to haggle. She read through the email one last time and then hit send.

There was only one thing left to do. She took a deep breath and picked up the phone on her desk. Her heart thumped in her chest as she listened to it ring one time, two times, three times. "Come on, pick up," she whispered. Finally, on the fourth ring, a man answered. She recognized the voice from their earlier conversation.

"Hi. This is Samantha Alwood again. I spoke to you earlier about the Dornea Pines property."

"Yes. I remember."

"I wanted to let you know that I have decided to make an offer on the property. I sent my offer in an email just before I made this call."

"Thank you for your call. I'll add your offer to the others that have come in this afternoon and let you know when the owner makes a decision."

Samantha felt as if someone had just hit her in the back of the head. "Other offers? Earlier you told me there were no offers on the property."

"Correct. At the time we spoke earlier, no offers had come in. Since then, we have received two. Three if I count yours."

"I see."

"I'll let you know what the owner decides as soon as possible."

"Thank you." Samantha hung up the phone and

dropped her head into her hands on top of her desk. If the home already had two offers, chances of her offer being competitive weren't very good—especially since she'd come in under the asking price. If she continued missing out on these good deals, she'd be looking for a new career before her current one even had a chance to set its roots.

After leaving the office that evening, Samantha decided to take another drive past Dornea Pines. As she drove through the dark streets of Provo, memories of similar October nights such as that one flooded her mind. She'd come home from school, finish her homework, and then sit on her front porch with her mom, sipping hot chocolate and watching the cars and people go by.

She loved her city and the neighborhood she grew up in. People decorated for all the holidays and especially for Halloween. As a child, she loved trick-or-treating and usually had her costume planned and prepped by the time school resumed in August.

She smiled to herself as she recalled running from house to house with her friends in a sugar-induced frenzy. They knew by heart the houses that gave the good candy and the ones not to bother with. The mystery came every time a new family moved to the neighborhood. She always wanted to be the first to knock on the door and know what her prize would be. Her adult years reflected her youth. She still wanted to be the one leading the way.

Samantha turned onto Dornea Avenue for the second time that day. Jack-O-Lanterns flickered on porches and strands of orange and black lights lined the walkways to the front door. Cuddly inflatable ghosts and smiling witches dotted the front yards of some homes while bloody ghouls and rotting corpses took up residence at others. With Halloween so close, it seemed everyone anticipated the night.

Samantha pulled her car over in the same spot she'd parked earlier with Megan. Everything looked different in the dark of night. She stepped out of the car, but then reached into the backseat to retrieve her jacket. Daytime temperatures were still bearable, but evenings were brisk. When the canyon winds blew, it could cut right through a person.

Samantha ran her hand along the slats in the iron gate. The padlock still remained firmly in place. "What are you hiding?" she whispered. In the dark, even less of the home could be seen. Instead of angled corners and rooflines, blurry shadows filled the space normally occupied by Dornea Pines. The only thing giving away its presence was the pale light coming from the moon overhead. If she didn't know a home was there, she would have believed the pine trees led to nothing but emptiness.

Samantha looked at the rock fence—at least eight feet high—and then down at her high heeled shoes. If she were still her sixteen-year-old self, she'd be scaling that fence to get a better look. Her older, slightly wiser self knew the risk of damaging her reputation in the business community if she were arrested for trespassing wasn't worth seeing the home. Slapping her palm against the rocks, she let a small growl escape her throat. She hated losing and that's exactly what she imagined was happening to her in that very moment.

The sound of a motor caught her attention and she turned to see headlights approaching from farther up the hill. As the car neared her position, it slowed and dimmed its lights. In the dark, it was impossible to see inside the windows of the car, but she continued to watch as it crawled past the property line. Something about the car seemed familiar.

"Is that..." Samantha muttered as she watched the car's taillights disappear around the next curve. "It is!" she hissed. She knew without a doubt it was the blue car that passed the home earlier in the day when Megan was with her.

A sudden chill cut through her jacket and she pulled it tighter, taking a step toward her own car. Before she could get any farther, though, the blue car's brake lights came on and it rolled to a stop just beyond the Dornea Pines property.

"What the..."

The car's lights indicated it was about to reverse. Her heart pounded and her legs felt stiff as she tried to move them, suddenly aware that she was alone on an almost deserted road.

The car began to back up.

With a cry, Samantha ran for her car. She fumbled with her keys, dropping them into the leaves littering the ground more than once before she managed to unlock her door and jump in. She turned the key in the ignition with one hand while the other speed-dialed Megan's cell.

"Megan!" she screamed into the phone before her assistant even said anything.

"Sam? What's wrong?"

"I'm at Dornea Pines. Remember that car we saw up her earlier? The blue one? It's back. And I think it's following me!"

"*What? Slow down. Are you sure?*"

"I'm positive! It drove past me and then turned around and then it started backing up. I'm freaking out!"

"*Don't just stand there, get in your car!*"

"I am in my car. I'm driving way over the speed limit down this road."

"*You're a single woman alone on a dark road. Don't let them catch up to you.*"

"I have no intention of letting them catch me."

"*Could you see inside the car? Do you know who's driving?*"

"Not at all."

"*Should I call the cops? Meet you somewhere? Tell me what to do,*" Megan said.

"I don't know. It's dark and I panicked so I called you. I thought I might need a witness if this person forces me off the road and attacks. You can be my witness that I went out fighting."

"*Don't talk like that. Are they still following you?*"

Samantha checked her rearview mirror. "I don't see anything. Maybe I lost them. I'm headed to downtown where it's busy. The last thing I intend to do is lead them to my apartment."

"*Smart girl. Call if you need me to escort you home or something.*"

In the light of the city, things didn't seem so bleak. "Thanks. I'm sorry I bothered you. I'm sure it was nothing—probably just someone asking for directions. You know me. I'm a bit dramatic."

"*Don't worry about it. My husband is still at work so I needed some entertainment anyway. I'll see you tomorrow.*"

Samantha hung up her phone and sighed as she pulled into the parking lot of a twenty-four hour grocery store. The parking lot was at least half-filled with cars, but none of them were blue.

Maybe the car driving by didn't really pose a threat, but one thing was certain to Samantha. No matter how old she got, Dornea Pines still stirred an unexplainable fear in her.

Chapter 3

Samantha walked into her office at exactly 11 a.m. the next morning. She'd made stops at three of her properties on her way to work, each in a different state of completion. Both assistants looked up when she entered.

"Destiny, the house over on Plum is ready for paint and carpet," she said. "And have you sent final color choices to Rob yet?"

"Yes. I got them to him a couple of days ago. The carpet is in stock and the paint will be waiting at the warehouse for Rob to pick up when he's ready for it," Destiny answered without any hesitation.

Samantha smiled. "Perfect. I knew you were golden when I hired you." She started to step into her office, but then turned, tapping her fingers on the doorframe. "Megan, any word on Dornea Pines this morning?"

Megan frowned and shook her head. "Not yet. Sorry. You got home okay last night. Right?"

"Got home okay?" Destiny raised her eyebrows. "You're not the partying type. What did you do?" She said it with a smile, but her words came out sounding accusatory.

"I didn't do anything. I stopped by the Dornea Pines property and there was another car there. I thought they might be following me, but I was wrong. It was just a stupid moment of me losing my mind. It won't happen again."

"Don't tell me things like that." Destiny shivered and wrapped her arms around her shoulders. "Especially this time of year."

"You asked. I answered," Samantha said.

Destiny stood and walked around her desk. "Hey, are you still coming to help tonight?"

Samantha raised her eyebrows. "Help?"

"Don't tell me you forgot. You promised."

Samantha pulled out her phone.

"No cheating." Destiny laughed and stomped a foot on the floor. "You can't check your calendar."

"Give me a hint then."

"It has something to do with a certain upcoming holiday..." Destiny paused, waiting for a response from Samantha, but it didn't come. "And kids..." she continued.

Samantha remained stoic.

Destiny frowned. "Seriously, Sam? How could you forget? This is really important to me and you promised you'd come."

A wide grin spread across Samantha's face. "I'm just messing with you. Of course I remember. Tonight is the night you want me to do something with pumpkins for the kids at the hospital."

Destiny sighed in relief. "Right. Meet at the

community center over on Bulldog at six. We'll decorate for an hour and then make the deliveries at the hospital."

"Got it."

"And Sam?"

"Yeah?"

"Try to have fun, will you? There will be lots of people there. You could make new friends...or meet a guy."

"Is that why you wanted me to come to this? Is this some twisted way to set me up on a blind date?"

Destiny shook her head back and forth. "No. Honest. I've just noticed that you don't really do much other than work. I thought you might like meeting new people."

"She's right," Megan called from her desk.

Samantha rolled her eyes. "I can take care of my social life, thank you very much. I'll be there to support you tonight, Destiny, but don't plan on me hooking up with anyone. It's not really my style."

"What *is* your style?"

"Never mind." Samantha closed herself inside her office and leaned against the door, covering her face with her hands. Honestly, she'd completely forgotten that she'd promised to help Destiny with her annual Pumpkins for Patients event. Each year Destiny gathered dozens of donated pumpkins and then rallied volunteers together to decorate them for patients in the nearby hospital. They delivered them the night before Halloween so they could be enjoyed on the holiday. She'd never helped with the project before, but always thought it a worthy cause—one of many that Destiny spearheaded.

She knew Megan and Destiny were right about her

social life, but didn't want to admit that to them. For the past two years she'd focused all her time and energy on getting Alwood Properties up and running. Making friends and dating were the last things on her mind. Now that things were becoming more manageable, the holes in her life were becoming more pronounced.

Megan had been married before Samantha even hired her and Destiny currently had a serious boyfriend. Most of her friends from high school and college were married and some already had children. But for her, time had stood still.

Samantha set her phone to ring in the outer offices where one of the assistants could pick it up and logged on to her computer. Answering emails was always the first priority of the day. She scanned the subject lines of all thirty-eight new emails before deciding which to click first. Thirteen could be deleted without further thought, eight could be forwarded to Destiny, and three could be forwarded to Megan. That left her with fourteen emails, most of which were newsletters that could be skimmed and filed or deleted accordingly.

Just as she opened the last of the emails, Megan called on the intercom. *"I'm sending a phone call over. It's about Dornea Pines."*

Heart racing, Samantha's hand hovered over the receiver, waiting for it to ring. Not wanting to sound too eager, she let it ring one and half times before picking it up. "Samantha Alwood here," she said as nonchalantly as possible.

"Ms. Alwood. I'm calling in reference to your offer on the property at 114 Dornea Avenue." It was the same man she'd spoken with twice the day before.

"Yes. Do you have any word from the owner yet?" Even though the act was childish, Samantha closed her eyes and crossed her fingers.

"*The owner has looked over each of the four offers and has accepted none of them. They asked that each person submit a new offer reflective of the fact that there are four offers on the home. No offers from new parties will be accepted until the four parties already involved are accepted or decline to continue. You have twenty-four hours to respond.*"

Samantha opened her eyes. Three other offers on the table wasn't an ideal situation, but she still had a chance at her dream property. "Thank you for your call. I will reconsider my offer and let you know my decision by the end of the day." She hung up the phone and drummed her nails on the desk. She knew the original asking price was too good to be true. She'd purposely offered something under the asking price. It was possible that the other two parties did the same thing, but then again, they could have offered over the asking price, knowing what the property's real value was.

Samantha stood and walked to the door, yanking it open in one quick motion. Megan and Destiny both tumbled through the door. "If you're going to eavesdrop, don't do it at a time of day when your shadows show under the door."

Ignoring Samantha's remarks, Megan jumped in. "Sam, don't hold us in suspense. Did they accept?"

"Not yet. They gave us twenty-four hours to resubmit."

"They didn't counter offer?"

Samantha shook her head. "There were three other offers on the place yesterday. Apparently we weren't the only ones who realized it would be a steal. They want all four of us to revise our offers and resubmit them within twenty-four hours."

"How much room do we have in the numbers?" Destiny asked.

"Honestly? I don't know. Without seeing the house..." Samantha's words trailed off.

Megan grabbed a notepad off Samantha's desk and scribbled something on it before stuffing it into Samantha's hand. "This is the absolute highest we can go and still earn enough profit to make it worth our while. You can up your offer by a small amount, or you can pull out all the stops and give them that number. You decide."

Samantha stared at the paper in her hands and thought of the mysterious home tucked behind the pines. If she didn't go for it, she'd never forgive herself. "Let's do it. I'm all in."

"You do realize that you invited the only person to ever fail beginning art to help you, right?" Samantha asked Destiny as she stared at the pumpkin in front of her later that night.

"Come on, I'm sure you're not that bad. Besides, this stuff is easy. You don't have to be a Picasso."

"Picasso I can do. Didn't he just put weird shapes and body parts all over the canvas?"

Destiny rolled her eyes. "You know what I meant."

Samantha dipped a paintbrush in green paint and pointed it at her pumpkin. "I'm just suggesting that you not judge me too harshly."

"Your concern is noted."

Samantha swiped the brush across the orange flesh. "Wouldn't this be easier if we just cut holes in the pumpkins like Jack-O-Lanterns instead of painting them?"

"Do you really think the hospital would let a bunch of rotting fruit filled with fire sit next to the beds of their patients?"

"Point taken."

"You know, you didn't have to dress up for this event. Most people came in jeans and t-shirts." Destiny motioned to the other tables.

Samantha looked down at her black pantsuit and gray heels. "I came straight from the office. I didn't have time to change."

"Fine, but try to look a little more relaxed. You're as stiff as a board."

"At least I came."

"And I'm grateful for that." Destiny stood from her chair and wrapped her arms around Samantha's neck in a quick hug. "Some more volunteers just walked in and I need to greet them. Try to contain your enthusiasm while I'm gone."

"It'll be hard, but I'll do my best." Samantha went to work, smearing more green paint across the surface of the orange mound in front of her. She sat at the end of a long table by herself. Her eyes roamed over the other volunteers in the room but she didn't recognize anyone there except Destiny. She'd made her business the focus of her life for so long, she didn't realize how unattached she'd become from other people and the community.

Okay. Starting tonight, I'm turning over a new leaf. At least once a week I will do something others would consider social. She scanned the room for someone to talk to, but everyone seemed to have come with another person. Her eyes fell on the newcomers Destiny chatted with by the doors. "Is that who I think it is...?" she whispered.

A white-haired man walking by looked up in surprise. "What did you say? My ears aren't as good as they used to be."

"Nothing. Just talking to my pumpkin," she said.

The man gave her a funny look and then hurried past.

Wanting to get a closer look, but not wanting to be seen herself, Samantha lifted the green-painted pumpkin to her face and peered over the top of it at the room's entrance. Her instincts were right. Kyle Shipton, rival home-flipper, stood next to Destiny. A woman with long dark hair flanked his side. *Of course his wife is beautiful. He needs a little arm candy to polish off his perfect look.*

Suddenly, as if they were operated by some unseen force, all three heads turned in Samantha's direction. Afraid of blowing her cover, Samantha lifted her pumpkin higher, completely blocking her head from view. She continued to hold the pumpkin there as she stood and crossed the room to the table set aside for finished pumpkins. Her eyes roamed over the more carefully decorated offerings, but she shrugged and added hers to the table anyway, keeping her back to the rest of the room the entire time.

"Samantha Alwood?" a voice spoke from behind.

She jumped in surprise, barely keeping her pumpkin from rolling off the table as she whirled around. "Kyle Shipton."

Kyle's lips turned up and he looked at her as if amused. "Umm...I thought that was you. You've changed your appearance, though. This is an entirely new look for you."

Samantha smoothed her slacks and blouse with her hands self-consciously, not completely sure what his facial expressions meant. "I do change my clothes on a daily basis. I thought that was the norm, but maybe I'm wrong."

Kyle didn't explain his comment further. "Sorry about the auction yesterday morning. I know you really wanted that property. We've all got to keep our doors open and employees paid though, right?"

"Right," Samantha said through clenched teeth. "You must have some crazy connections to come in at such low bids." She knew he'd never offer up his secrets, but it was worth a try.

"I'm sure you've got your own favorite connections," he said with a sly grin. "There're plenty of properties out there for both of us. Of course, I'll take first pick of them and you can have my leftovers."

Samantha glared, but didn't say anything.

His wife slapped his arm. "Kyle, that's just mean."

Kyle grinned. "It was a joke. We always joke with each other, right?"

"Sure," Samantha said. No way was he joking—he just didn't want his wife to realize he wasn't as nice as she probably assumed.

"Cassie, this is Samantha. Samantha, this is Cassie." Kyle gave the introductions. The two women nodded at each other, but that was the extent of their interaction.

"I'm going pick out a pumpkin to decorate. Try not to embarrass me while I'm gone," Cassie said before flipping her hair over her shoulder and bouncing off in the opposite direction.

Samantha wanted to leave, but Destiny would kill her if she snuck out before helping with the pumpkin deliveries. "I guess I better start another one." She turned away from Kyle, her body stiff. Something about him set her on edge. But strangely enough, she didn't hate that feeling.

With a fresh pumpkin set before her, she went to work, daring to use more than one color and finding the task more enjoyable than expected.

"Mind if I sit?" Kyle stood across the table from her.

Back again? What is wrong with him! "Go ahead. I think your wife is at that table in the corner, though." Samantha nodded to the opposite side of the room.

Kyle's head jerked up. "My...wife?"

Samantha nodded.

Kyle's face flushed ever so slightly, but then he laughed. "You mean Cassie? She's not my wife. She's my sister."

"Oh. Sorry."

"It's fine, but now I'm wondering how many other people have thought that. We do hang out a lot. This could explain why I have such a hard time finding a date."

"Or it could just be your personality," Samantha teased.

"Ouch."

"You deserved that one for beating me at another auction."

"Okay. I'll give you that."

Samantha reached for the blue paint at the same time Kyle did. Their hands touched briefly and they both looked up in surprise. Samantha felt a tingle she hadn't expected, at least, not from Kyle.

"Sorry. You use it first," he said, pulling away.

"Thanks."

"So...what's new for Alwood Properties?"

Samantha thought of Dornea Pines and almost told him about it, but stopped herself. A fellow home flipper would appreciate the good deal, but she didn't want to tip him off on something that wasn't yet hers. "Same old grind. You?"

"I have one home that should be finished next week and three more that will be done within the next month. And now I've added the new one from yesterday's auction. Sometimes I wonder if I'll ever catch my breath."

"You found time to come here tonight."

"Cassie made me. Something about not getting out enough."

Samantha laughed, knowing that Destiny had told her the same thing earlier that day. "Sounds familiar. Well, this pumpkin's finished. I guess I better take it to the drying table. Nice talking to you." She didn't know if she meant it, but it felt right. The conversation had definitely been better than ones in the past.

Kyle leaned back in his chair and turned on his charming smile—the one he always used at auctions. It fooled most people, but not her. "You, too. See you at the next auction, if you're still in business."

Samantha glanced at the pumpkin in her hands, tempted to throw it at him, but she took a deep breath and let it go. Acting like a child wouldn't make a difference, but beating him at his own game would. And that's exactly what she intended to do when she acquired Dornea Pines. It would be her masterpiece flip.

"Sam, what happened to you?" Destiny's eyebrows

creased as she watched Samantha set her pumpkin on the drying table.

"What do you mean? I'm just dropping off another pumpkin. I told you I'm not very good at this whole painting thing."

"I saw you flirting with the enemy over there." Destiny's eyes flitted to the pumpkin on the table and then back to Samantha's face. Her strange look remained.

Samantha's jaw dropped. "I was *not* flirting!"

Destiny put her hands up in defense. "Whoa. It was a joke. Of course, only a guilty person would get that upset over a joke."

Samantha ignored the comment. "I'm tired. Isn't it time to deliver these yet?"

Destiny continued to stare at Samantha's face. "Soon, we're just waiting for a few people to finish. I think maybe you should take a break. You know, freshen up."

"Why would I want to do that? I'm just going to go home and get in my fuzzy pajamas and drink some hot cocoa."

"Trust me." Destiny nodded. "The restrooms are over there." She pointed to the back of the room.

With a sigh, Samantha trudged off in the direction of the women's restroom. She stepped inside just as another lady was leaving.

The woman took one look at her and grinned. "Looks like you're having a lot of fun tonight."

"Why is everyone acting so weird," Samantha mumbled as the door shut behind the woman.

She stepped in front of the mirror and gasped. Her forehead, both cheeks, and part of her nose were smeared with bright green paint. "What the...I don't understand." She'd been so careful not to get paint on her tailored suit, how did it get on her face?

"Kyle," she moaned. When she'd lifted her pumpkin—in an attempt to hide from him when he arrived—she must have smeared the wet paint. No wonder he'd made comments about her appearance.

Samantha leaned in and touched one of the green smears on her cheek. "My life is over. I can never show my face in public again."

Chapter 4

"Y ou're here early," Destiny said when Samantha walked into the office just before nine the next morning.

Samantha leaned her open umbrella against the wall and unbuttoned her coat. "I went to the Butterfly property to make sure Hardy was still on schedule, but it started raining and I didn't want to traipse through there with muddy shoes. I'll have to check it later today."

Destiny opened the blinds on the window next to Megan's desk. "Is it still pouring out there? I thought it was starting to slow down."

"I think the storm got its second wind." Samantha headed toward her office, but then stopped and took a closer look at Destiny. "Nice hair."

"You like it?" Destiny giggled and patted the top of her head. Her normally dark locks were streaked with bright orange.

"Uhh...define what you mean by like."

"Don't worry, it's only temporary. It matches my

clothes." Destiny lifted her long black skirt to reveal orange plaid leggings underneath. "I love Halloween! You should have dressed up."

"I thought you hated being scared," Samantha said.

"Oh, I do. I just like any holiday. And I like the cute princess and fireman costumes, not the bloody gross ones."

"Oh. Well, I did dress up. I brought my black umbrella rather than the red one."

Destiny picked up a rubber band and flipped it, but Samantha easily ducked and it soared over her head. "Megan texted me on my way in and said she was running behind this morning, but she'll stop and get hot chocolate for all of us if you promise not to be mad."

Samantha's jaw dropped. "When have I ever been mad at either of you?"

"Never. I think she just needed an excuse to get hot chocolate."

"I don't mind that. I'll be in my office, praying for a miracle at Dornea Pines."

"Still haven't heard anything?"

"Not since yesterday. They said they'd make a final decision today, though." As if on cue, the phone began to ring just as she finished her words.

Destiny grabbed the receiver from its base. "Alwood Properties, Destiny speaking." Silence. "Uh huh. Okay. She just came in. I'll transfer you to her line now." Destiny quickly punched a couple of numbers on her phone and set the receiver down. "It's them!" she hissed.

The phone in Samantha's office began to ring. She rushed into the room, pushed the door shut, and dropped her coat onto a chair. She managed to grab the phone on its third ring and slide into her chair all in one motion. "Samantha Alwood." She sounded slightly out of breath.

"Yes. This is Richard Hargrave. I've spoken to you a couple of times over the last few days regarding the property at 114 Dornea Avenue."

"Yes, Mr. Hargrave. I'm hoping you're calling with good news for me."

"I'll let you be the judge of whether the news is good or bad. I was calling to inform you that two of the other parties involved withdrew their offers last night. You and the remaining party both sent in new offers yesterday."

"And..." Samantha drummed her fingers on her desk nervously.

"Your offers were identical to each other."

Samantha's heart fell. "And now you want us to submit again?" She couldn't take much more of the waiting game.

"No. Actually, the owner is—" Mr. Hargrave cleared his throat, "a bit eccentric."

"I guess that explains why we aren't allowed to see the property."

"Correct. The owner has decided that both offers are acceptable and wishes to decide between you and the other party in what she has determined to be a fair test."

The conversation was not going the way Samantha expected. Not by a long shot. "What sort of test are we talking about?" She'd been out of college for three and a half years and test taking had never been her forte.

"The owner has suggested that you and the other party visit the property to make sure it's what you really want."

Samantha breathed a sigh of relief. "Finally. I would love to see what I'm trying to buy. Blind purchases make me nervous."

"*There's more.*"

"Of course there is."

"*You are welcome to spend as much time looking inside the home and around the grounds as you like.*"

"That sounds generous."

"*But, you will view the property with the other interested party.*"

"Still sounds doable. I'm not sure I'm seeing the bad angle to this."

"*The first of you to leave loses the property.*"

Samantha's heart felt like it skipped a beat. "Excuse me?" He had to be joking. He got Halloween and April Fool's Day mixed up.

"*Believe me; I know it sounds like an odd situation. Did I mention the owner is a bit eccentric?*"

"It came up."

"*She insists this is the best way to determine who wants the property the most.*"

"I can save her the hassle. I want it the most."

Mr. Hargrave chuckled. Up to that point, he'd been nothing but serious and Samantha had started to wonder if he was human or robot. "*Are you available tonight? The owner wishes to be finished with this transaction as soon as possible.*"

Samantha thought of her evening plans. If it went like every other Halloween since she'd been living alone, she would watch old horror movies on TV and try to convince herself that they didn't scare her. She would hand out candy to the no more than a dozen children who ventured through her apartment building in their costumes and then end up going to bed with the lights on. Seeing the inside of Dornea Pines on Halloween ranked much higher. "Absolutely. What time should I arrive?"

"Be at the gate no later than seven and I will escort you in."

"Perfect. I look forward to it."

"Uhh...Ms. Alwood, I suggest you bring an overnight bag with you. I called the other party first this morning and they informed me they once stood in line for four days to get concert tickets. I don't think they'll back down easily."

"Thanks for the heads up. I think I can handle them, though. Am I allowed to bring anyone with me?"

"Only yourself. The other party must come alone, too."

"Got it. I'll see you at seven."

Samantha opened her office door. Destiny glanced up from her computer and Megan, who must have arrived while she was on the phone, jumped up and came toward her with a Styrofoam cup.

"So? Is it good news?" Megan asked as she handed over the cup. "I'm trying to decipher your facial expression and I can't."

"I...I'm not sure. You're never going to believe the conversation I just had."

Samantha stood in the bedroom of her small apartment, staring into her closet. Richard Hargrave had warned her to bring an overnight bag. He sounded serious, too. She didn't want to give her opponent—and that's what she thought of the other party involved—confidence by bringing too much stuff and appearing needy. On the other hand, she wanted the person to know she wouldn't back down easily. If she looked as if she intended to stay awhile, they might give up and go home.

"This is by far the strangest thing I've ever done," she muttered as she pulled a large black bag off an upper shelf in her closet and began tossing toiletries into it. She wouldn't take a change of clothes, but she would bring the essentials—like a toothbrush and a good book. She moved to the kitchen next and added a water bottle, energy bars, and a couple apples. "Most importantly, my cell charger," she muttered, as she dropped the cord into the bag. *If this madness lasts too long, I'll just call Megan or Destiny and have them slip me some stuff through the gate.*

Heading back to her room, she slipped out of her skirt and blouse and into jeans and a sweater. She traded her high heels for sneakers. The rain from that morning had stopped, but she intended to explore the grounds of Dornea Pines and it would be muddy from the earlier storm. Looking professional was the least of her worries that night. Samantha glanced at her watch. 6:25 p.m. She had just enough time to grab a sandwich at her favorite deli and still make it to Dornea Pines by seven.

The sun slipped behind the mountains beyond Utah Lake as she drove down University Avenue, one of the main roads cutting through town. She pulled her car into an empty space in the parking lot of Simon Says Subs and ran into the building.

"I'd like a number three on wheat, please," she said. The clerk nodded his head and went to work behind the counter. The sandwich had turkey and avocado with a thick smear of cranberry sauce. Her favorite, she stopped for it at least once a week.

She dropped the paper sack from the deli inside the black bag sitting on the passenger seat of her car and continued on her way to Dornea Pines. Children in costumes of all shapes and sizes filled the sidewalks of the residential areas. Each of them carried a sack, plastic pumpkin, or pillow case bulging with the evening's haul.

"The dentists in town will be busy in about a month when all of that's gone," Samantha whispered to herself with a smile. Memories of trick-or-treating as a child again flooded her mind, bringing waves of nostalgia. She longed to relive those memories. *Maybe it's time for me to think seriously about joining Megan in the married category. In a few years I could have a little witch and fireman of my own.* The thoughts surprised her.

Samantha's car traveled up Dornea Avenue as if it knew the way there. The twists and turns of the road felt familiar after the last couple of days. An annoying commercial came on the radio so she reached down to change it to another station. Her eyes were only off the road for a moment, but when she looked back up, a black cat stood in the road directly in front of her.

"No!" she screamed as she slammed on her brakes. She closed her eyes as her car skidded to a stop just feet from the animal. The cat didn't seem the least bit bothered by the fact that it almost lost its life and sauntered off toward the left side of the road. "Let's hope that wasn't an omen," Samantha whispered as she looked at her bag that slid to the floor when she slammed on her brakes. She'd have to scoop it up when she got to the house.

The few other homes on Dornea Avenue were

more lit up than the previous night, probably for the sake of small children in the area, but the entrance to Dornea Pines was just as dark and foreboding as ever. This time, a gray four-door sedan idled in the spot where she'd parked on her other visits. She pulled in behind it and turned off her engine, pulling the keys from her ignition. A man stepped out of the car in front of her and came toward her.

"I'm Richard Hargrave," the man said, extending a hand. "You must be Samantha Alwood."

Samantha took his hand and shook it. "You're correct. It's nice to finally meet you." She smiled to herself, but forced the laugh trying to escape back down her throat. Richard Hargrave looked exactly as she'd pictured him. Late fifties or early sixties, bushy eyebrows, and a stern look that not even a baby kitten could crack. She imagined him as the butler of Dornea Pines, opening the door for anyone who managed to make it past the gates. The image brought another laugh and she turned toward the fence so he wouldn't see her grin.

"What happens if the other party doesn't show up?" Samantha asked.

"I wouldn't count on that happening, but I guess you'd get to have the tour all by yourself," Richard answered.

"And then what? Do you have the contracts ready to sign? I'm available right now."

"Patience, Ms. Alwood. The other party will be here."

As if on cue, the sound of a car approaching caught both their attentions and they turned away from the gate to watch its arrival. At first, the headlights shone in her face and she raised a hand to her eyes to shield them from the light, but as it pulled onto the shoulder of the road on the opposite end of the gate, her heart began to thump in her chest. The car that parked and cut its engines was the same blue one she'd seen twice the day before—the one she'd run from after she foolishly thought it was following her during a moment of weakness. *Please don't let it be anyone creepy.*

"I believe this is the other party," Richard said, motioning toward the car.

The door of the blue car opened and a black shoe emerged. Judging by the size and shape, it belonged to a man. The full body that unfolded itself from the car made her jaw drop. The man shut his door and a grin spread across his entire face.

"Hello, Samantha."

Kyle Shipton.

Chapter 5

"Y ou have *got* to be kidding me," Samantha hissed when she saw who emerged from the blue car.

Kyle shut his car door and took a few steps forward. "I see you came to look at my house again. This makes what...three times?"

"Your house? I'll be the one signing for the title of this property. Mark my words. You will not win this time." Samantha crossed her arms over her chest. "If you saw me looking at this why didn't you say anything last night? You were trying to get me to say something, weren't you?" she accused.

Kyle opened his mouth to say something else, but Mr. Hargrave cut him off. "I see that the two of you already know each other. I guess that saves me introductions and thirty valuable seconds of my time. Now, if you don't mind, I'd like to explain the rules and be on my way. If I'm gone too long on Halloween night, I'm afraid my house will be covered in eggs when I get home. That's not something I feel like cleaning up tomorrow."

Samantha suppressed a smile and focused her attention on Mr. Hargrave. Kyle leaned against the hood of his car and continued to grin.

"The rules of this transaction, as set by the owner, are that the party who stays on the property the longest will have their offer accepted. You may go anywhere you desire in the house or on the property as long as you are respectful of the owner's belongings and take responsibility for any damage you may cause. While you are a guest at the property known as Dornea Pines, you will not invite or allow anyone else on the property. If you do, your offer is forfeited. Make absolute sure that this is the right fit for you while you are here tonight. When one of you is ready to leave, call me and I will unlock the gate so you can retrieve your car. The other party will then have their bid officially accepted by the owner of the property."

Mr. Hargrave stopped to clear his throat and looked from Samantha to Kyle. "I hope that after tonight, at least one of you is still interested in purchasing this place. I'm not sure I want to continue with these silly games. Good luck."

Samantha's eyes narrowed. "You don't think we'll want the property after we see it?"

Mr. Hargrave shrugged. "I cannot speculate on that. I do not know either of you well enough to know your likes or dislikes." He inserted a key into the gate's lock and unwound the chain from around its slats. As he pushed it open, the metal squeaked and creaked as if it hadn't opened in ages.

The groaning of the gate twisted Samantha's stomach into knots and she wondered if she was about to make a big mistake. *Should I back out? This whole thing is getting kind of creepy.* One look at the smug smile on Kyle Shipton's face and she had her answer. She'd be staying at Dornea Pines until he gave up or she keeled over and died.

"Let me grab my bag and lock my car," Samantha said. She circled her car and retrieved the black bag from the floor where it had fallen when she slammed on her brakes to avoid hitting the cat. As a last minute thought, she opened the glove compartment of the car and dug through it until she found her emergency flashlight. Being prepared might be the difference in her winning or losing the battle.

"All set?" Mr. Hargrave asked as she and Kyle crossed through the gate. Both parties nodded. "Great. Enjoy your stay." He started to swing the gate closed.

"Wait!" Samantha stuck her arm out and stopped the gate's progression. "You're not coming up to the house with us? How are we supposed to get in?"

Mr. Hargrave tugged on the gate until it latched and then clicked the padlock into place. He stuck an arm back through the slats. "Here's the key to the house. If I were you, I'd lock the door behind myself."

Kyle reached for the key, but Samantha grabbed it before his fingers reached Mr. Hargrave's.

"I'll take that," she said. "It's going to have a permanent home on my keychain soon anyway."

Kyle dropped his arm, but didn't say anything. They both watched in silence until Mr. Hargrave's car disappeared down the hill.

"So," Kyle began. "What's with the creepy butler guy?"

Samantha laughed. "My thoughts exactly. He would fit well in this house. I'm surprised he doesn't just buy the place himself."

"Do you know who the owner is?"

Samantha shook her head. "He didn't tell me. Do you know?"

"Nope. All I know is that Mr. Hargrave is acting as middleman. I did an internet search for the name and he seems to be a local lawyer."

"I didn't know what their relationship was, but that would make sense."

"Have you seen this home before?" Kyle asked.

"Not the inside."

"Same here. My assistant called me as soon as this home was listed a few days ago. I was in the vicinity so I drove by. The portion I could see from the gate piqued my interest, but I didn't know what the entire home was like. I figure it must be pretty bad if we had to make our offers without seeing it."

"I saw the full home as a teenager once. The outside that is, not the inside."

"Really? Did you know someone that lived here?"

Samantha tilted her head and peered at Kyle. "I take it you're not from this area."

"What makes you say that?"

"Anyone who grew up in Provo knows about Dornea Pines."

"You caught me. I'm actually from the Logan area."

Samantha looked in the direction of the house, but couldn't see much in the dark. "Dornea Pines has a reputation for being haunted."

Kyle raised his eyebrows in surprise. "You're kidding, right?"

"No joke. And I'm not just trying to scare you away. Although, if that's what it takes to get you to back out of your offer, then yes, there are dozens of ghosts running amok in the home."

"The fact that it has a questionable past makes me want it even more."

"Somehow I figured that would be your answer." Samantha sighed. "Back to your original question, teens used to sneak up here now and then, and especially on Halloween, to get a picture by the home. A few claim they actually made it into the home, but I never saw any proof."

"Did you ever try?"

"There used to be a shorter fence around the property. My friends and I climbed it once, but as we got closer to the house we realized a light was on inside so we ran off."

Kyle smiled. "I didn't picture you as the trespassing type. There's an entirely different side of you that I need to contemplate."

"No offense, but I doubt you know *anything* about me."

"I could say the same for you. Although, I'm pretty sure you have a strong opinion of me nonetheless."

Samantha lifted her shoulders and then dropped them again in a deep shrug. "You're my biggest competition in town. Of course I have an opinion of you. Should we head toward the house?"

Kyle swung a backpack onto his back. "After you."

Samantha eyed his bag. The bag she'd chosen was slightly bigger and definitely fuller. From the looks of it, he didn't pack much. Score one for her.

Tall pine trees flanked both sides of the driveway leading to the house. Beyond the single row of pines, leafy trees in all their autumnal glory covered the rest of the acreage. Walking through the trees made Samantha feel as if she'd been transported out of Provo and into a woodland dream.

"You look different, by the way." Kyle broke the silence between them.

"Different? What do you mean? And is that good or bad?"

"I've never seen you without high heels and business attire. I would have never guessed that you owned a pair of jeans."

"You spend time thinking about my wardrobe? Isn't that a little strange...even for you?"

"Okay, I deserve that one." Kyle put a hand up. "I never thought about it until last night. I've never seen anyone show up to a pumpkin painting party all dressed up like you were."

"I had to go to the party straight from work so I didn't have time to change and I didn't want to disappoint my assistant who was running the entire thing," Samantha said all in one breath. "Since I can't seem to win any new auctions, I've got to put extra hours in on other projects."

They continued walking in silence, but Kyle couldn't handle it. "So, I see your makeup job is back to normal today. Last night's facial was...interesting."

The green paint from the pumpkin. Samantha felt her face turning red and put a hand to her cheek, thankful for the dark. "It wasn't—"

"Oh wow." Kyle stopped walking and let out a low whistle. The trees had just opened up and the entirety of Dornea Pines could be seen. "This is not at all what I expected."

"Out of curiosity, what did you expect?" Samantha asked.

"For the price they were asking, I figured it would be an old home with a caved in roof and fire damage. I based my offer on property value only."

"Same here." Samantha glanced back the way they came. Only a tiny corner of the gate could be seen. Once they hit the front door it would be completely hidden. "There's still time to be disappointed. The inside might be rotted out."

"There's only one way to find out." Kyle nodded toward the house. "I believe you're holding the key."

Samantha took a deep breath and walked up the steps of the wide front porch. They groaned beneath her, but seemed to be solid. Her heart beat faster as she inserted the gold key into the lock of the solid wood door. She held her breath as she turned the handle and pushed it open. They stepped over the threshold together and silently took in their surroundings.

"Hello?" Kyle called.

"Are you expecting the ghosts to answer?" Samantha smirked.

"You never know. Mr. Hargrave didn't specifically say no one lived here, did he? Maybe the owner is hiding out in the attic."

"If the owner is hiding in the attic, I doubt she will answer your call of welcome anyway. Besides, Mr. Hargrave told me she was eccentric, not insane."

Not much could be seen in the dark, but two distinct doorways led to rooms on either side of the entry. Samantha stepped forward and through the doorway on her right. The faint moonlight coming through holes in the tattered curtains didn't provide much light. She patted the wall on either side of the doorway, but couldn't find a light switch. Before she could say anything, a sudden brightness filled the room and she blinked a few times in surprise.

"The bulb still works," Kyle said, his hand still holding the pull string of a floor lamp.

"Thanks."

In the light, the entirety of the room could be seen. Once a formal sitting room, all that remained of the furnishings besides the lamp were an old, paisley-print settee and two hard-backed chairs. The walls were covered in textured wallpaper the color of avocados. A stone fireplace with a mahogany mantle spread across the back wall.

Kyle rubbed his hand along the back of the settee. "The good news is the home isn't caving in. The bad news, it hasn't been updated...ever."

"No, but maybe that's actually good news. If the history of the home is well preserved, it might entice my buyers to spend more when I put it on the market," Samantha said.

"You meant to say *my* buyers."

"No. You heard me correctly." Samantha pulled her black bag from her shoulder and set it on one of the chairs. She dug through the contents and pulled out two things—a measuring tape and the turkey sandwich she'd already forgotten existed. The bread the deli used smelled like heaven when she unwrapped the sandwich and took a bite. She thought about offering half to Kyle, but figured the hungrier he got, the quicker he'd cave.

Instead, she sat in the chair and 'Mmmed' and 'Ahhed' over every bite of the sandwich. When only a few bites remained, she looked up at Kyle. "Oh, I'm sorry. I'm being rude. Did you want some?"

Kyle put his hands up and shook his head before taking up residence on the settee. "I filled up before I left home. I'll be good for a long time. Days, if necessary."

Samantha crumpled the sandwich wrappings and tossed them into her bag. Then, taking the measuring tape with her, she walked to the window and stretched the tape out along the width of the room.

Kyle leaned back against the cushion of the settee and crossed his arms over his chest as he watched her. "What, may I ask, are you doing?"

"Measuring."

"I figured that much out on my own."

"Then why did you ask?"

Kyle reached down and grabbed the measuring tape.

"Hey! Give that back." Samantha lunged for the tape that Kyle held over his head, but his height advantage would never let her reach his arm. Instead she pretended to punch him in the gut and when he flinched, bringing his arm down, she grabbed the measuring tape.

"You're so stubborn." Kyle laughed. "Will you please just explain to me why you're measuring the room?"

"I want to know how much space my contractors will have to work with. I'll be texting them numbers tonight."

Kyle jumped back. "Hold on a minute. This house isn't yours yet."

"Exactly. It's not mine *yet*."

Kyle rolled his eyes. "We're not allowed to let anyone else in. If you break the rules, you forfeit the house to me. I'm not going to let you cheat if it puts me at a disadvantage."

"I'm not letting anyone in. I'm just passing the information along." In all honesty, she didn't have any intention of texting anyone that night, but Kyle didn't need to know that. The more she could psych him out, the better.

"Well, while you're playing house in this room, I'm going to explore the rest of my castle."

Not wanting to miss anything, and still feeling a little weirded out in the old house, Samantha tossed the measuring tape back into her bag, flipped off the lamp, and followed him into the room across the entryway.

"A music room, maybe?" Kyle asked after he turned on a lamp matching the one in the sitting room.

"It looks that way. The price of the home included furnishings, right?" Samantha asked as she fingered the keys on an old upright piano. She didn't know anything about musical instruments, but in her mind it was in great condition—once you got past the thick layer of dust.

"Right. Although I'm surprised they're leaving some of this stuff." Kyle sat on the piano bench. "Maybe this item will entice buyers to spend a little more." He stretched his fingers and then began to play a slow, haunting melody. It fit perfectly with the home's ambiance, but it sent chills up Samantha's spine.

"That music is depressing," she said.

"Do you prefer something more upbeat?" Kyle asked as he started in on a fast-paced song. "Or is there something else you want to hear? I take requests."

"Show off."

"Have you ever had lessons?"

"Never."

"You at least know *Chopsticks* though…right?"

Samantha turned away. "I told you, I've never had a lesson."

"Everyone knows the song, even if they haven't had lessons." He grabbed her arm and gently tugged. "Sit down and I'll teach it to you. It only takes a minute."

Samantha eased herself onto the bench next to Kyle. Her goal for the evening was to convince him that she was competent and capable—competition rather than someone to crush—but musical talent had always escaped her. She tried learning to play the flute her first year of junior high, but gave up after one semester. The next year, she signed up for choir, but couldn't hit any of the notes. Every time they had a test where she had to sing for the conductor, he'd frown and shake his head in pity. She only passed the class because participation points made up three-fourths of the grade. Attempting to learn a song on the piano would only end in one-sided laughter.

"I really have no musical abilities," she insisted.

"You don't need musical abilities to play *Chopsticks.*"

"Just don't laugh, please."

Kyle grinned. "I'll try to contain myself." He rested his fingers on the keys and then played a few notes, one finger at a time. "Now it's your turn. Copy what I just did."

Samantha took a deep breath and put her hands on the keys. Kyle adjusted her fingers to the right notes. "Here goes nothing," she whispered.

After a few fails, she eventually mastered what he'd played and he showed her the next part of the song. Five minutes later, she could play the entire song, jabbing at the keys with one finger on each hand. "I'm doing it!" she squealed. "This is fun."

Kyle laughed. "Just keep playing. When you get to the end, start over again. I'm going to join in."

Samantha did as instructed and Kyle began playing a more complicated accompaniment on the keys above her. Then, he jumped up and slid onto the bench on the opposite side and began playing a deeper tune.

Samantha giggled. "Are you making it up as you go?"

"Maybe a little," he answered as he reached around her back and played the high notes with his right hand while his left continued to play below her.

The feel of his arm against her back broke her concentration on the keyboard and she stumbled over the notes, tried to catch up, and then gave up and put her arms in the air. "Enough!" She laughed.

"See, I knew you could do it."

Samantha stepped around the bench and put a safe distance between them. "That was fun. Thanks for my first piano lesson."

"Anytime."

A floor to ceiling bookcase filled one wall of the music room. Most of the shelves were bare, but a few dusty books remained. None of them looked as if they'd been read in the current century. Near the piano, an old electric organ loomed, as if watching over everything else in the room.

"Do you think this thing still works?" Samantha asked.

"Only one way to find out." Kyle reached behind the organ and plugged its cord into an outlet.

Samantha pressed a few buttons, but no sound

came out. "Nope. That's probably why they left it here. Too lazy to take it to the trash."

Kyle reached around her and pushed a button. The organ lit up and a faint hum filled the room. "It helps if you turn it on."

Samantha tested a few of the keys, but it still didn't produce sound. "Still nothing."

Kyle tapped a few of the keys. "I guess this will be one of the first things to go when I start renovating this room."

"When *I* start renovations, I'll just have my guys drop it off at your place. I'm going to need your address."

"Nice try." Kyle walked toward the doorway. "I'm going to keep looking around. You coming?"

Samantha turned the lamp off and followed him back to the entryway. A narrow staircase led to the upper floor and a hall continued further into the house.

"Which way?" Kyle asked.

Samantha pointed down the hall. "Let's finish this level first."

The hall led to a small kitchen and dining area. There were no table and chairs and the hardwood floors were warped and cracked. "Here's the first big expense," Kyle said.

"And if you pull up the floors, what else will you find," Samantha added.

"My thoughts exactly."

They couldn't find a lamp in the kitchen and the overhead light had burned out bulbs, so they used their cell phones to take inventory of the room. Samantha busied herself by opening cabinet doors and looking at empty shelf after empty shelf. The pantry mimicked the cabinets.

"Hey, did you know this place has a basement?" Kyle asked.

Samantha followed the sound of his voice to the back of the dining area. Kyle stood at the top of a steep staircase, shining his cell light into the dark hole.

"Is it a basement or just a cellar?" she asked.

"Not sure. Want to check it out?"

"Sure, but I'm not going down there with only cell phone light. I've got a flashlight in my bag. Let me grab it first." Samantha hurried back down the hall to the sitting room where she'd left her bag. The flashlight was the emergency type that didn't require batteries so she had to wind the handle for a minute before the light came on. "Perfect," she whispered.

A sudden loud noise coming from across the hall jarred her and she whirled around to face the doorway. Kyle must have returned to the music room, but Samantha couldn't understand why he kept playing the same note over and over. "Kyle?" she called.

Silence.

"Kyle?"

When he still didn't answer, she marched into the hall, grumbling, "What is he doing in there?"

Kyle stood in the hallway. "What's going on?"

Samantha aimed the flashlight at him. "I was going to ask you the same thing. Are you trying to wake the ghosts?"

Kyle blocked the beam of light with his arm and turned his head away. "I'm not doing anything. But, if you're out here...who's in there playing the organ?"

Chapter 6

Samantha's knees felt as if they were made of rubber. She didn't know which sound was noisier—the incessant organ notes or her own heart beating in her chest. "Kyle, this isn't funny."

"Samantha, I swear I didn't do anything."

"You can't scare me off like this."

"For the millionth time, I'm not trying to. I heard the noise from the dining room and came to see what you were doing."

Samantha and Kyle both turned toward the music room. Convinced she'd see an opaque woman in century-old clothing sitting on the bench, Samantha clutched the arched doorframe before stepping into the room. "Who's in here?" she called. From the doorway, the organ filled the room with a hazy light, but its bench sat empty.

"I don't get it," Kyle said, turning on the lamp again. They both turned in circles, looking in all directions and peering into every corner, but they remained the only souls in the room.

Samantha approached the organ. "One of the keys is pressed. I think it's stuck."

Kyle punched at the key a few times, but it didn't stop playing. "Just turn it off."

Samantha reached around him and pushed the power button he'd pushed the first time they were in the music room. The sound immediately stopped, but her ears continued to ring. "How did it do that in the first place?"

Kyle shook his head. "I'm not sure. If I had to guess, I'd say it took the organ that long to warm up. Since the key is broken, it started to play as soon as it was able. Did we leave it on?"

Samantha raised and then dropped her shoulders. "I think so?"

"That's the explanation I'm going with. Anything else would be ridiculous...right?"

Samantha smiled. "Right."

Kyle motioned toward her hand. "I see you found your flashlight. Ready to explore the basement?"

Not sure she was ready to go into a place like that before her heart had a chance to recuperate, Samantha said, "Actually, let's finish the rest of the downstairs first. There're still a couple of doors we didn't open and the glass door led to a sun porch."

"Works for me."

On the way to the kitchen, they opened two doors. One led to an empty coat closet and one led to a half bath that didn't look like it had been used in the last fifty years.

Kyle opened the last unopened door on the first floor. "Hey, this is a den. There's an old roll top desk and chair." He stepped to the side so Samantha could see around him.

The room felt colder than the rest of the house and Samantha shivered. "What a depressing room. There's not even a window in here." She backed out of the room and pushed on the glass door leading to the sun porch. It swung open, revealing rotted wicker furniture and dead plants in planters of all shapes and sizes. At some point in time, that little room on the back of the house must have been a vibrant focal point of the house. Samantha couldn't wait to get her hands on it and return it to its original beauty.

They paused in the dining area long enough to wind the flashlight again, neither wanting to get trapped in a dark cellar without any light. "Tell me about your family," Samantha said as she leaned against the wall and watched him twist the handle around in a circle. She could tell a lot about a guy from the way he talked about his family.

"What do you want to know?"

"I met your sister...Cassie was it?"

Kyle nodded.

"Any other siblings?"

"More than you could imagine. There are eight of us altogether."

"*Eight*? Are your parents crazy?"

"I've wondered that, but no. They're great. Things could get a little chaotic when all of us were home, but we always had someone to hang out with. Now that I've been on my own for a while, I kind of miss the noise."

"Where do you fall in the lineup?"

"Third. Cassie is fourth. She's dating a guy pretty seriously right now. I predict they're engaged by

Christmas. He had to work last night so she dragged me to the pumpkin painting event with her."

"Do you want a big family of your own?" Samantha asked.

"Everyone always asks me that when they find out how many siblings I have, but I'm never sure what to answer." He sighed. "I want kids, but I don't know how many. That's something I should discuss with my future wife before making any decisions, don't you think?"

Samantha laughed. "I'm sure whoever she is, she'd appreciate having some say in the decision."

The flashlight glowed bright and steady. "You ready to head down?"

"Lead the way."

The steep steps leading to the basement—or cellar as they decided to call it—were made of cement and so narrow that they had to descend sideways to keep from falling forward. "I'm glad I don't have to go up and down these things on a regular basis," Samantha said. She didn't dare hold too tightly to the handrail for fear it might give way and send her tumbling to her death.

At the bottom of the stairs, Kyle found a cord hanging from the ceiling and pulled. An overhead light switched on. "Would you look at that," he said. "The only room in the entire house that has working overhead lighting and it's the dingy basement. Who would have thought?"

Samantha giggled. "It was probably built by a man."

Kyle whirled around. "You better watch what you say. I can easily unscrew the bulb and I don't think you're tall enough to screw it back in." He took a step back. "I also happen to be holding the flashlight. Think how easy it would be to turn it off." His eyes betrayed him as they sparkled in the light and his lips twitched as he fought to hold back a smile.

Samantha took a step closer and then lunged for the flashlight. Kyle yanked his hand out of reach just before her hand closed on the light.

"You'll have to try harder than that." He grinned.

"Too bad I chose to leave my high heels at home. A swift kick to the shin would be appropriate right about now," Samantha said as she lunged for the flashlight again. Kyle moved his hand *and* took a step back. Her momentum threw her off balance and she fell forward. Kyle grabbed her and held her around the waist. She stood upright. Their faces were only inches apart. Both were flushed and glowing. Embarrassed, Samantha started to pull away, but Kyle squeezed her shoulder before releasing her.

Samantha blushed and her entire body felt tingly—something she hadn't felt in a long time. *Do not let yourself fall for him. He's the enemy. And there's a good chance seducing you is part of his plan to win the house. Keep your head in the game.* She cleared her throat. "So, what crazy things are hiding down here in the basement?"

"Unless you consider a very outdated washer and dryer to be crazy, you're going to be disappointed," Kyle said as he shone the light around the room.

"I'm more concerned about the extent of renovations needed. When I'm flipping a house and the basement looks as if it's had a lot of water damage, or the foundation is cracked, or there's mold...it's not a good sign."

"True. And I *can* hear dripping somewhere." The

pair followed the dripping noise until they found the source—a leaking pipe. "I'll have to have someone look at it, but I don't think this will be too much of an issue. I really feel like the bones of this house are still good."

"That's how I feel, too. I can't wait to get started on *my* renovations."

Kyle twisted to look at her. "You're going to take every opportunity that you can to remind me I don't get the house yet, aren't you?"

"No. I'm going to take every opportunity I can to remind you that you don't *ever* get the house."

Kyle threw his head back and laughed. "There's the Samantha I know."

She nodded toward the stairs. "Want to return to the land of the living? I think we've seen everything there is to see down here. The room can't be more than a hundred square feet...max."

Back upstairs, Kyle handed the flashlight to Samantha. "Now what?"

"Nothing left but the upper floor. Maybe we'll finally find some ghosts up there."

Kyle motioned to the hall. "You have the flashlight so I'll let you lead the way."

"What's the matter? Chicken?"

Kyle grabbed the flashlight out of her hand and stomped toward the staircase. "I don't mind going first," he called over his shoulder, "but you better keep up since I have the light."

Samantha followed close behind as he ascended the polished wood staircase to the second level. On the landing at the top, they both paused. Kyle moved his arm toward the closest room. "I think this is a bathroom. Want to check it out?"

"Sure."

Inside, a pedestal sink and a claw foot tub were the most interesting fixtures. Samantha turned the handle on the sink and a stream of water came out. "Does the toilet flush?" she asked. Fixing the plumbing could be costly—not to mention the fact that she might need to use that particular appliance before her stay at Dornea Pines ended.

Kyle pulled a cord dangling from the ceiling and the toilet flushed.

"Thank goodness," Samantha mumbled.

The pair explored three bedrooms and another bathroom on the same floor, but all were empty of any and all furnishings. Mousetraps in the closets were the only thing worth mentioning. The traps were empty, much to Samantha's relief.

"On to the next door," Samantha said after leaving one of the empty bedrooms. She reached for the knob of a door at the end of the hall, but it wouldn't turn. She looked at Kyle. "I think this one is stuck."

"Let me try." He handed the flashlight to her and twisted the knob. "It's not stuck. It's locked."

Samantha pulled the house key from her pocket and tried to insert it into the lock, but it didn't fit. "This is the only key Mr. Hargrave gave me. What do you think is in there?"

"Dead bodies?" Kyle joked.

"You're hilarious."

"Honestly, it probably leads to the attic. I doubt there's anything but junk up there."

Samantha nodded toward a door on the opposite wall. "We still have one more bedroom to look in."

Kyle pushed the door open. "This room is furnished."

Samantha followed him in, aiming the flashlight into the room. "This is amazing!" She turned on a lamp next to the bed and tucked the flashlight into her back pocket. "All of these pieces have to be at least a hundred years old." She ran her fingers along the headboard and up one of the posts. "Kyle, the bed was hand carved."

Kyle stepped toward her and leaned his head in to inspect the bed. His fingers brushed against hers as he felt the carvings in the post. Embarrassed, they both pulled away.

Kyle pulled the curtains aside and glanced out the window. "The view of the city alone is worth every penny of the owner's asking price. You can see all the way over Utah Lake from up here."

Samantha joined him at the window. "Everybody lights up on Halloween. It makes the city seem huge."

"Got to keep the spooks and ghouls away."

"Or the egg throwers, as Mr. Hargrave pointed out." Samantha took a step back and her hand brushed against something on the nightstand next to the lamp. She sucked her breath in sharply. "Kyle...look."

Kyle dropped the curtain and focused his attention on her. "What is it?"

Samantha handed him a cream colored envelope. "It has my name on it."

Chapter 7

Kyle stared at the envelope Samantha handed him for a moment before lifting his head. "And it was just sitting there?"

Samantha nodded and handed him another envelope. "There's one with your name on it, too."

"Why does this make me nervous?"

"I don't know, but I feel the same way. You open yours first."

Kyle sat on the edge of the bed and tore the envelope open. He pulled out a single sheet of paper. "It's a letter."

Samantha sat down next to him and slid her finger along the seal of her envelope. She pulled out a matching sheet of paper. "Want me to read it out loud?"

"Go ahead."

"*Dear Potential Homebuyer,*

Welcome to Dornea Pines. This home has been in the Dornea family for more than a century. You stand in a room that has been the site of many happy occasions as well as many that are heartbreaking. As the last living Dornea heir, I have made the sad decision to sell the home. I hope that whoever purchases the home and property will give it the respect it deserves— from the walls of the home to the unique pines to the family burials on the south side of the property.

"This home was erected in 1897 by Erastus F. Dornea. He lived here for six happy years, planting trees—including the pines lining the road to the house—and hosting many friends and family members for parties and socials. He succumbed to the effects of liver failure just shy of the home's sixth anniversary. His widow, Diana, mourned his passing and shut herself in her room—the room where you now stand—for many months before finally being coaxed out by her pride and joy, her youngest son Coleman. Every time he left the home, she'd withdraw to her room, only coming out when he was present. Tragedy struck when Coleman passed while serving as an officer in World War I, once again throwing Diana into a tailspin. She died only days after hearing the news of Coleman, presumably of a broken heart.

"I tell you this story not to make you feel sorry for the Dornea family, but to make you understand that this property has a spirit of its own. The home has passed from family member to family member for generations, but no owner has kept it long. The estate has a way of pulling even the strongest down to its darkness. Perhaps if Dornea Pines is inhabited by someone not of the Dornea lineage, the 'curse' will be broken and happiness can once again return. If you are the last to stay at Dornea Pines, and your offer is accepted, take this home and make it your own. Let the* *happiness return.*

"*Sincerely, The GGG-Granddaughter of Erastus F. Dornea*"

Samantha finished reading the letter and carefully folded the paper, returning it to its envelope.

Next to her, Kyle cleared his throat. "That was a little intense."

"No kidding. Is she trying to sell us the house or talk us out of it?"

"That's what I wondered." Kyle leaned forward and rested his elbows on his knees. "There was something that stood out to me in that letter, though."

"What?"

"Are there really burial grounds on the property?"

Samantha felt a chill run through her. "I think so. Growing up, it was rumored that there were some graves on the property. I figured it was just another made up thing to make people believe the place is haunted."

"Do you think the graves are marked?"

Samantha shrugged. "You know as much as I do."

"I say we go find them."

Samantha's stomach tightened. She didn't usually frighten easily, but the dark feeling described in the letter was real. She felt it. But Kyle couldn't know that. She glanced at her watch. "It's nine thirty. I guess if we're going to go, we should do it before it gets too much later."

Samantha switched off the lamp and followed Kyle out of the room and down the stairs.

"I have to admit, you're smarter than me. I wish I'd packed a flashlight," Kyle said as they both stepped outside. The beam from Samantha's little flashlight didn't stretch very far.

Samantha gasped. "Can I get that recorded and notarized, please? Kyle Shipton admitted of his own free will that I'm smarter than him."

"I'm confident enough in my own abilities to admit when others are good at something I'm not." Kyle stopped at the bottom of the porch stairs and looked at Samantha. "The letter said the burials were on the south side of the property. Which way is that?"

Samantha pointed. "South is back toward the gate we came in on. It must be in one of the corners."

"Through the trees it is."

The pair stayed close together as they pushed their way through the trees. "So," Samantha began, "what brought you to Provo? Did you come just to make my life miserable?"

"I went to school at UVU and never left. I like it here. Besides, there are a lot of houses people have given up on in this area. I enjoy the process of taking one man's trash and turning it into a true home."

"That's how I feel. There's something magical about each transformation."

"And the paychecks aren't bad either."

Samantha laughed. "Yeah. There's that. Bills have to be paid somehow, right?"

"I told you about me, now tell me about Samantha Alwood. What makes her tick?"

Samantha turned and looked at him, trying to judge his expression, but it was too dark to really read him. "Well, for starters, my best friends call me Sam."

"Is that an invitation?"

"We'll see how the night progresses. Anyway, my dad was in real estate. I got my love of the business from him. He didn't do a lot of property flipping, but that's where I've put my emphasis. He retired a couple of years ago and he and my mom spend most of their time traveling now."

"Any siblings?"

"Two. Both brothers. One lives in California and one in Colorado. Neither of them followed in Dad's footsteps."

"Is that bad or good?"

"I'm not sure how to answer that. It's good, I guess. They both followed their own dreams. Sadly, their dreams took them away from here, but that's fine. They did what is best for them. We have a blast when they come for visits—usually when my parents are going to be in town for a while."

"You're lonely."

Samantha's heart fluttered. She hadn't meant to spill so much of her personal life to Kyle Shipton, the man she was supposed to be at war with. Maybe this was his way of trying to break her down. But, if she was honest with herself, his two word accusation was one hundred percent correct.

When Samantha didn't answer, Kyle cleared his throat. "I'm sorry. That was rude."

"No. It's fine. I—" She didn't get to finish her thought. Her foot caught on a rock in the dark and she stumbled forward. Kyle caught her just before she hit the ground. "Thanks."

"No problem. Here," he said as he offered his arm.

Samantha hesitated before taking it. *This is so not how I expected to be spending my evening. I'm supposed to hate this guy, but I can't find anything wrong with him. I need to dig deeper like he did with me.*

"I think we found it," Kyle said, pulling her from her thoughts.

Smooth, round stones formed a square around several weathered headstones. Grass and weeds grew in tall clumps around the markers, but even in the dark, the headstone shapes were undeniable.

"Let me see the flashlight," Kyle said as he took it from Samantha's hands. He pushed a clump of grass away and aimed the light at the nearest marker. "Erastus F. Dornea, 1832-1903."

Samantha knelt next to the headstone. "Seventy-one years old. I'm surprised he built such a big house at his age. I mean, he would have already been in his sixties when they moved in, right?"

"Right. Maybe he knew he wouldn't last long and wanted a nice place for his wife to live out her final days. Or maybe he intended it to be passed down from generation to generation. The home was his legacy."

"Maybe..." Samantha scooted to her right and cleared debris from another headstone. "Coleman Dornea is buried here next to his father," she said as her fingers traced the words. "It says he lived from 1875 to 1918—killed in the Battle of Belleau Wood."

"Does that mean anything to you?" Kyle asked.

Samantha shook her head. "I enjoy history, but I don't know much about the first world war."

"Same here."

They carefully made their way across the damp ground, clearing stones and reading names and dates off four additional headstones. Each of the stones listed Dornea as the surname, but didn't give any indication on the person's relation to the original owner. All four deaths occurred after Erastus died, but before Coleman.

Samantha stood and used the flashlight to look around the tiny cemetery. Its beam fell on a tall stone set in the back corner of the plot. "There's another headstone back there. Why wouldn't it be up here by the others?"

"Maybe it's not a close relation. Or maybe it's the black sheep of the family. Admit it. Every family has someone they'd like to hide."

Samantha knelt by the headstone and brushed away the fallen leaves covering the base. The wind blew her hair around her face and she had to keep tucking it behind her ears in order to see clearly. She sucked in her breath when she saw the name on the headstone. "It's Diana."

Kyle knelt next to her. "1847-1918," he read. "Poor lady. She wanted to be left alone in her room while she was still alive, maybe she wanted to be left alone in death."

"Maybe. It just seems...sad." Samantha picked up a dried bouquet next to the marker. The dead flowers were tied with a dull yellow ribbon. "Someone left her flowers, but from the looks of them, they've been here awhile."

A strong breeze whistled through the trees and cut through Samantha's thin jacket. She wrapped her arms around her chest and shivered. "Anything else you want to see while we're out here? If so, we should hurry. I smell rain again and I'd rather not get caught out here in it."

"I agree." Kyle stood and offered his hand to pull her up. "Let's start heading back." He took a step forward and then stopped. "Sam," he said, shortening her name. "When we were done reading the letters in the upstairs bedroom earlier, you turned the lamp off before we left the bedroom, right?"

What a strange question. "I did. I specifically

remember doing it," Samantha insisted. "Why?"

Kyle pointed through the trees toward the house. A light shone in the upstairs window. "I don't think we're alone at Dornea Pines."

Chapter 8

Samantha gasped and covered her mouth with her hands. The flashlight fell to the leaf-covered ground. "This is a joke. You did this somehow." Her voice shook.

"I swear I had nothing to do with it. I left the room first, remember? That's why I asked if you turned the light off," Kyle insisted.

"I know I did. I remember doing it. Kyle, someone's up there."

"You locked the front door when we came out. Is there any chance you dropped the key when you were done?"

Samantha lowered her hands from her mouth and felt for the key in the pocket of her jeans. Just as she knew they would, her fingers grasped the gold key to the front door. "No chance. It's in my pocket still."

"That means someone was in there with us the whole time."

Samantha cringed. "No wonder I kept having the feeling someone was watching me."

Kyle raised his eyebrows. "You did?"

"Maybe a little."

"Why didn't you say something?"

"And make you think I was scared of the house? No way."

"Listen, Sam, I'm not trying to nor do I intend to try to sabotage you. I promise. If I'm going to win this place, I'm going to do it fair and square. Got it?"

He called me Sam again. She nodded.

"Good. Now I say we go back up to the house and sneak up on whoever is in the room. It's probably just the owner, come to check on us."

"Which owner? The one who currently owns it or Diana?"

Kyle raised his eyebrows. "*Now* you believe it's haunted?"

"I'm being open minded."

Kyle bent down and picked up the flashlight Samantha dropped in her moment of panic. "Let's kill the light so whoever it is doesn't see us coming."

Much to Samantha's surprise, Kyle grabbed her hand and led her through the maze of trees. Something like that should have felt awkward and foreign, but it didn't. Her hand fit perfectly in his and she savored the warmth it provided. The pair stumbled multiple times as they fought their way through the trees in the dark without the help of the flashlight, and she was grateful for his steadying hand. They stood in the shadows of the pine trees and watched the home for a few moments.

"Do you see anything?" Kyle asked.

Samantha shook her head. "Just the lamp."

"Let's do this."

They darted across the lawn and up the front

porch. Samantha handed the house key to Kyle and glanced at the upstairs window. The light flickered as if a shadow passed by. "It's just my imagination," she whispered.

"What did you say?" Kyle asked quietly as he let go of her hand long enough to slip the key into the door lock.

"I thought...nothing."

He tilted his head at her, but didn't say anything. "The inside stairs squeak so we'll have to be careful," he whispered as he slowly pushed the door open.

Samantha stepped across the threshold after him. The wind caught the door and slammed it shut behind her. She cringed. "I think we just announced our arrival."

Kyle put a finger to his lips and motioned for her to follow him. She stayed close to him as they ascended the stairs, easing her weight from foot to foot, one step at a time. They hesitated at the bedroom door, pressing their ears to the wood and listening for hints of who or what might be on the other side.

"Do you hear anything?" Samantha whispered.

Kyle shook his head. "I'm going to throw the door open on the count of three."

Samantha nodded and lifted her head from the door as Kyle held up one...two...three fingers. He turned the doorknob and pushed on the door all in one movement. The two tumbled into the room with their hands up in defense, but then stopped short at what they saw. The lamp was turned off.

Samantha grabbed her flashlight and flipped it on. The light flickered and turned off. She wound it again, wishing they'd thought to charge it before they entered the room. Her heart pounded in her chest, but she was grateful Kyle stood next to her. When the light's full beam came on, she turned in a slower circle, aiming the light deep into every corner and under the bed. "I know that lamp was turned on just a minute ago. You saw it, too," she demanded.

"Shh." Kyle pointed toward the closed closet door. "Whoever it is must be in there."

Samantha stopped talking and watched as he stepped carefully across the bedroom rug. She braced herself, not sure she wanted to see what would fly out of the closet. As the door flew open, Samantha aimed the light directly into the space. Nothing. The closet was just as empty as the ones in all the other bedrooms.

Samantha dropped her arm and flopped down on the bed. "I don't understand. None of this makes any sense. I *know* that light was on just a minute ago."

Kyle shut the closet door and sat down next to her on the bed. "Could the light have been a reflection of something else? Headlights maybe?" He reached over to turn the lamp on, but as he touched the table, the lamp came to life. "Hey, did you see that?"

"See what?"

"I didn't turn it on. It did it by itself."

"I saw you stick your arm out."

"I know, but I didn't turn it on. I think there's a short in the plug." Kyle reached forward again and nudged the nightstand. The lamp flickered and then turned off. "I don't know if it's the bulb or the plug or what, but I don't think anyone was in here."

Samantha hesitated. "What about the shadow?"

Kyle jostled the table again and the lamp turned on. "Shadow?"

Samantha cleared her throat and drummed her

fingers on the bed nervously. "When we were on the porch, I looked up at the window and saw a shadow cross in front of the window."

Kyle narrowed his eyes. "Are you sure?"

"Pretty sure."

"We were able to explain away the organ playing by itself and the lamp. There's got to be a way to explain a shadow." He stood and turned in a circle as if searching for something. "Did the shadow have an outline, like a person, or was it more fluttery?"

Samantha closed her eyes and tried to remember. She only saw it for a second before moving beneath the porch roof. "Maybe more on the fluttery side."

"That's what I thought." Kyle reached forward and moved the curtains back and forth. "Is this what you saw? It's been getting windier outside and you know these old homes are drafty—not to mention the fact that the curtains are super thin. They could have easily moved."

Samantha sighed. "I'm sure you're right. I guess I overreacted." Deep down she knew Kyle's explanation was right, but for some reason, it left her feeling disappointed. Part of her wished the home really was haunted...and for the life of her she couldn't explain to herself or anyone else why.

The letters the current owner left for Samantha and Kyle still sat on the dresser. Samantha folder her envelope and tucked it in her pocket. She wanted to remember the story of Erastus and Diana so she could preserve its memory when she flipped the home.

"We've covered the house and the south side of the property. Anywhere else you want to go?" Kyle asked as a clap of thunder rattled the house. The lamp turned off again and they both laughed.

"I'm not in the mood to get soaked and I have a feeling it's about to start pouring. I'd rather wait to see the rest of the property when it's light and dry." She rubbed her fingers along the edge of the bed, picking at stray strings on the mattress. "I guess this is the part where we part ways and see who can survive the longest. We've seen the house, we both still want it, there's nothing we can do but wait."

Kyle looked down at his hands and then stood. "You're probably right." He stuck his hand out as if wanting to shake. Samantha took it and he squeezed hers with a firm grip. "It's been fun, but now it's time to get serious. As a gentleman, I'll let you take this bedroom since it's the only one furnished. I'll sleep on the sofa in the sitting room."

"Are you sure? It's not very big."

"I don't mind. I doubt I'll be sleeping much anyway. The storm is noisy and the walls here are thin."

"Thanks. I appreciate it."

Kyle stepped toward the door, but Samantha stopped him.

"I'll come down with you and get my bag." She started to follow him, but then reached behind the nightstand and yanked the lamp plug out of the wall. "We wouldn't want any more false alarms.

Sitting on the bed in the upstairs bedroom, Samantha felt unusually alone. She'd had her own apartment for years and never felt like something was missing until she shut the bedroom door, closing herself off from the rest of the house—and Kyle. She patted the mattress and a cloud of dust floated up. Sleeping on it would wreak havoc on her allergies. It didn't matter, though. Just like Kyle, she doubted she'd be getting much sleep, especially without any bedding.

A shiver reminded her that although she'd worn a sweater *and* a jacket, she was still cold. She rubbed her hands up and down her arms as she crossed the room to the ancient radiator. Kneeling on the floor, and putting all her weight into it, she managed to turn the valve on the appliance. "Now, we'll just hope it still works," she muttered. The clanks and bangs coming from the pipes and vents were a welcome sound. If anything 'went bump in the night,' she could just blame it on the radiator.

Outside, the thunder and lightning increased in intensity. Samantha left the radiator and pulled the curtains back, tying them on each side. The view of the storm from the upper floor of Dornea Pines couldn't be matched anywhere else in Provo and she considered inviting Kyle up to watch it with her.

As a child, she'd kneel on her bed and peek between the slats of her bedroom blinds to watch the storms. Her brothers usually left their rooms, too scared to sleep anywhere but their parents' bedroom floor, but not Samantha. She lived for the storms. That night, all she needed was a comfy chair and a bowl of popcorn and the evening would be perfect.

After a few minutes of rumbles and flashes, rain began to patter on the window and everything outside became blurred and hazy. Samantha's eyes drooped and she swayed in place. The room had warmed significantly. Maybe the dusty mattress wouldn't be so bad after all.

She pulled her cell phone from her pocket and checked the time. "Eleven forty-five," she whispered. *I thought for sure it was at least three. This night is taking forever.* With one last glance at the storm, Samantha reached to untie the curtains. But something stopped her. She leaned forward, pressing her face against the cold glass. *My imagination is still on overdrive. I didn't see anything. There is nothing out there. Kyle and I are the only ones on the property,* she tried to convince herself. But as she stared out the window, she knew it wasn't true. An orb of light bobbed up and down in the trees, coming ever closer to the house. It couldn't be Kyle out exploring. He didn't have a light. Someone...or something...was wandering around the property.

Chapter 9

S amantha sucked in her breath. "I've got to tell Kyle." She grabbed the windup flashlight off the nightstand and stuffed it in her back pocket.

The radiator sent out a whistle just as she yanked the bedroom door open and she jumped in surprise. She didn't want to give away her location to anyone outside so she kept the flashlight turned off and instead ran her fingers along the wall as she crept down the hall toward the stairs. She grasped the handrail tightly and took one careful step after another until her feet scraped the hardwood floors at the bottom. She tiptoed into the sitting room and squinted at the settee. It didn't look like anyone was there. "Kyle?" she whispered. "Are you asleep?"

Nothing.

"Kyle?" she said again, louder that time.

Still nothing.

She stepped forward until her knees bumped against the settee and ran her hands along its empty fabric. The little light coming from the dwindling storm outside proved that both chairs were empty, too.

Knowing that the intruder could be entering at any moment, she darted across the entryway to the music room, hoping he'd decided to sleep in there instead. "Kyle!" she called. "Kyle!" Feeling the panic rising from the pit of her stomach, she left the music room in search of a place to hide. "Kyle!" she yelled one last time. From behind, someone grabbed her by the shoulders and she screamed, convinced her life would end that night.

"Sam, calm down. It's me."

The hands turned her around and in the dim light she recognized Kyle. "It's you." She sighed in relief.

"What's wrong? You sounded scared." The concern in his voice was genuine.

"I...I didn't know where you were." Staring into his eyes, her worries didn't seem as serious as they had only moments before. She tried to pull away from him, but he held her tight.

"I was in the bathroom. You know, nature called."

"Kyle, we're not alone here."

"Huh?"

"I was looking out the upstairs window and I saw a light floating around. Someone's on the property and they're headed this way."

Kyle opened his mouth as if to say something, but he stopped when the doorknob behind them rattled.

Samantha stopped trying to pull away and clutched his arm, her nails digging into his skin through his long-sleeved shirt. "See, I told you!" she hissed.

Kyle stared at the knob as it rattled on the door. "Did you see who it was?"

Samantha shook her head.

"What if it's Mr. Hargrave?"

"He would have called first. We've got the key, remember?"

Kyle pried her fingers from his arm and pulled her with him into the sitting room. "Maybe we can see the porch from the window in here." The curtains were partially open, leaving a one foot gap to view the outside world. Kyle leaned against the window and peered through the opening. A grin replaced the worried expression.

"What is it?" Samantha whimpered. "What do you see?"

"What did you tell me you already knew about this house? Something to do with Halloween?"

She narrowed her eyes and shook her head, not sure what he meant.

"You told me you'd only been to Dornea Pines one other time in your life...and it was on Halloween."

Recognition struck and a smile crossed Samantha's face. "Teenagers?"

"Bingo. There's at least five or six of them out there. They're taking pictures," Kyle said as he continued to stare out the window.

"Let me see."

Kyle stepped aside and Samantha took over his spot in front of the window. From the entryway, the doorknob continued to rattle as each teen attempted to break into the house. "How did they get over the fence? It's at least two feet higher than when I was growing up and it was hard enough back then."

"Kids are inventive. Or maybe they brought a ladder."

"Should we call the police?" Samantha asked.

"I don't know. I'm sure it's just a harmless dare."

"Yeah, but if they do any damage, the owners are going to blame us. And I'd rather not have more things to fix once the deed to the house is in my name."

Kyle laughed. "You never give up, do you?"

"Never."

Kyle looked out the window again and then took a step back. "You know," he began, "we could have a little fun with them if you want."

"Meaning..."

"Meaning we scare them off the property."

A smile crept onto Samantha's face again. "Keep going."

"They're here because they've heard rumors that this place is haunted, right?"

"Of course."

"Let's give them even more reason to believe in it." He turned his head back and forth and then snatched a crocheted doily from off the back of the settee. "Here," he said, tossing it at Samantha. "Go to the bedroom facing the front of the house and put that over your face. Count to thirty and then turn your flashlight on. It'll make it seem like you're a ghost standing in the window. I'll stay here and bang on the door from the inside. If they don't pass out, they'll get off the property faster than you can get back downstairs."

"You're a genius," Samantha said. She grabbed the doily and darted for the stairs. "Ready?" she called over her shoulder. "One...two...three..." She counted as she ran up the stairs and back down the hall, its familiarity leading her to the room where her black bag still sat on the bed. No longer afraid of the home, she burst through the door and crossed to the window, breathing hard. "...twenty-seven...twenty-eight...twenty-nine...thirty!" With the doily covering her face and her arms at her side, she turned on the flashlight, aiming it up toward her face.

From the floor below she heard a thunk, followed by another thunk. They came in rhythmic succession, one after another. Outside, the teens' screams could be heard through the closed windows. Samantha fought to stifle the laughs, but finally gave in, knowing a shaking ghost would only make the prank better. She counted as five or six bobbing flashlights disappeared down the lane toward the gate.

"That was awesome!" Kyle said, bursting through the door a moment later.

Samantha turned away from the window, still aiming the light at her face. "Oooooo!" she hummed.

Kyle collapsed onto the bed. "No wonder they ran so fast. That's pretty realistic in the dark."

Samantha turned off the flashlight and tossed it onto the nightstand before pulling the doily from her face. She sneezed twice from the residue the cloth left behind. "I'm wide awake now." She laughed. "Thanks a lot."

"My pleasure. Did you see the kid who fell?" Kyle asked, still laughing.

Samantha shook her head.

"I watched through the peephole. They were tripping over each other, trying to be the first to get off the porch. One kid actually fell off the porch." Kyle could barely talk from laughing so hard. His laughter only made Samantha's worse and before either of them knew what was happening they were lying on the bed in fits of giggles.

Samantha wiped her eyes and sat up. "I can't remember the last time I've had this much fun on Halloween...or the last time I've laughed this hard."

"Me neither. Being a grownup is hard sometimes."

"I do miss the innocent days. We could do as we wanted as long as we showed up for class during the school year. Bills and mortgages and insurance and all the joys of adulthood weren't even in our vocabulary."

Kyle rolled onto his back and crossed his arms behind his head. "Tell me about your teenage self."

"What do you want to know?"

"Were you the studious kind who always had her nose in a book and never went out on the weekends? Were you the life of the party and the leader of the crowd? Were you athletic? Were you the star of every school play?"

Samantha tucked her knees into her chest and leaned back against the headboard. "I'd have to say I fell into a couple of those categories. I got decent enough grades, but I preferred to fly by the seat of my pants for most of my classes. I don't think I was the life of the party, but I definitely liked to party. Athletics were not my thing. They still aren't. I have a gym membership, but that's the extent of it. My membership card gets pushed to the bottom of my purse more often than not."

Kyle leaned on one elbow and looked up at her. "That's not what I would have guessed."

"You thought I was athletic?" she asked, surprised.

"No. I mean, I've never really thought about it, but judging by your seriousness at auctions, I would have pegged you as the studious girl who stayed home on the weekends to cram for tests that were still two weeks away and turned down all dates because she didn't want a boyfriend to interfere with her college plans."

Samantha's jaw dropped. "What? I don't give off that impression."

Kyle didn't say anything.

"Okay, maybe I'm serious at auctions, but that's a place I *should* be serious. That doesn't mean I don't like to have fun." Honestly, Samantha couldn't remember the last time she'd gone out just to have fun. Even attending Destiny's pumpkin painting party had felt like a chore and she only went out of obligation.

"Are you mad?" Kyle asked.

"No...it's just...I didn't realize I'd changed so much." She dropped her knees and crossed her arms over her chest. "What about you? What was Kyle Shipton like as a teenager?"

"I—"

"Wait!" Samantha put her finger over his lips. "Let me guess first."

"Go ahead."

"You were the student body president, captain of the debate team, and you ran on the cross country team. You didn't quite make valedictorian, but you were in the top ten of your graduating class. You made sure everyone knew who you were."

No sound came from the other body on the bed.

Samantha cleared her throat. "Did you fall asleep?"

"No."

"Did I guess anything right?"

"Some of it..." Kyle hesitated. "I was number twelve in my graduating class and I was on the debate team, but I wasn't the captain."

"What about the rest?"

"There's a good possibility that I was the student body president...and that I was on the cross country team."

Samantha couldn't hold back her laughter. "Ha! I knew it. I had you pegged right from the beginning."

"What did you mean by the other part?"

"What other part?"

"You said 'I made sure everyone knew who I was.'"

Samantha turned away and picked at the piping along the edge of the mattress. "I didn't mean anything bad; I just meant that you were an attention seeker."

Kyle remained quiet.

"Are *you* mad?" she asked quietly.

"No. I just didn't know I came off that way. I don't necessarily want attention. Is it so wrong to want to be successful?"

Samantha shook her head in the dark. "No. I know the feeling. Sadly, as of late you have become much more successful than me, but..."

"And then I rub it in your face, right?" Kyle said.

"Uh huh."

"I'm sorry."

"I've done my fair share of taunting I'm sure. Being a woman in this field, I feel like I always have to prove something."

"If it makes you feel any better, I consider you my biggest competition. None of the men out there scare me like you do."

Samantha smiled down at him. "Thanks. It does make me feel a little better, actually."

Kyle pushed himself up with his arms and stood. "It's almost one thirty. We've made it six and a half hours so far. It's been fun, but I should probably let you have your bedroom back. Truce?"

Samantha stuck her hand out and took the one he offered. They shook, but neither pulled away. Instead, they held on for a few extra seconds—seconds that ticked by as if in slow motion. "Good night," Kyle finally said, pulling away first.

"Good night."

Samantha sneezed. And then she sneezed again. And then, again. Falling asleep on the dusty mattress in the only furnished bedroom at Dornea Pines was not one of her finest moments. She opened her eyes, but couldn't see anything. She fumbled for her cell phone on the nightstand and checked the time. Four o'clock. She'd managed to sleep for a couple of hours. She stretched each limb, starting with her legs and moving to her arms before twisting her head and neck back and forth.

Wide awake, Samantha knew she wouldn't be able to fall asleep again. She needed a distraction. She reached behind the nightstand and plugged in the lamp, making sure the plug was secure in the outlet so there wouldn't be any repeats of the light-in-the-window-incident.

She glanced around the room, looking for something to do, but found nothing. "What did I pack," she muttered as she turned her black bag upside down on the bed and watched the contents spill out on the dusty mattress. She sifted through the debris for a minute before grabbing an apple and a novel she'd started reading the weekend before. With apple in hand and head resting on the back of the bed, she tried to read. Between the flickering light, the uncomfortable bed, and the noisy radiator, she couldn't concentrate. She slammed the book closed and tucked it back inside her bag. *If I don't find something to entertain me, I'm going to throw in the towel long before Kyle*. When she'd agreed to staying at the house, she didn't realize just how little there would be to do.

"Maybe Kyle's awake," she mumbled. If he still slept, she could always go back into the music room and explore what few items remained on the bookshelves.

She unplugged the lamp again and turned down the radiator before crossing the hall to the bathroom with the claw foot tub. The water wouldn't heat up, but she splashed some on her face anyway and dried her face on her sleeve. She brushed her teeth and rinsed her mouth, relishing in the clean feeling. *Good thing it's dark everywhere*, she thought as she stared at her hazy image in the mirror.

Leaving the bathroom, she turned toward the stairs, but then stopped in her tracks. Something wasn't right. Something had changed. Not sure she wanted to look behind herself, she counted to ten before turning around slowly. Her eyes had not played tricks on her.

The door to the attic was ajar.

Chapter 10

Samantha hesitated in the hallway. She didn't know how and she didn't know why, but the attic door had somehow opened. Most of her brain told her to go downstairs and wake Kyle, but the other part reminded her that she'd already raised false alarms about the organ, the light in the window, and the mysterious light coming through the woods that turned out to be teenagers on a dare. The last thing she wanted or needed was Kyle thinking she was scared of everything. There had to be a simple explanation for the open attic.

With her head held high and her shoulders back, she marched down the hall toward the door. Light glowed through the small opening between the door and the doorframe. Samantha grasped the knob and pulled. The door creaked as it scraped across the floor. Inside, a narrow staircase led toward the unknown. Samantha drummed her fingers on the wall and looked over her shoulder, trying to muster enough courage to keep going. *You can do this. It's no big deal.*

She moved her right foot forward, placing it on the bottom step, and then shifted her weight to move her left foot onto the next stair. *See, you're doing it. You're moving. I knew you could do it.* The third stair groaned when she stepped on it and she hurried to the fourth. Each step took her closer to the top and closer to unfamiliar territory.

"Hello?" she whispered at the top of the stairs. "Is someone up here?"

From behind an old armoire, a head popped up. Samantha screamed.

"Sam! It's me."

"Kyle? What the...how did...what are you *doing* up here?" Samantha leaned against the wall and slid to the floor. "I think I just experienced a heart attack."

Kyle hurried from behind the boxes and crouched down next to her. "In my defense, you *did* call out and ask if anyone was up here."

"I didn't expect anyone to answer."

"Sorry."

Samantha laughed. "Now that my heart has started beating again, I guess it's kind of funny."

"I'm glad you can find the humor in it."

Samantha turned her head from side to side, taking in her surroundings. "How did you get in here? I thought the door was locked."

Kyle sat down on a box next to her. "I couldn't sleep—no surprise there—so I decided to take another look around the study downstairs. I opened all the drawers in that old secretary and found this." He paused in his explanation long enough to reach into his pocket. Out came a small key. "I had nothing better to do so I decided to see if it fit the lock to the attic," he said as he leaned forward to show Samantha the key. "It fit."

"How long have you been up here?"

"Not that long. Maybe five minutes. Did I wake you up?"

Samantha shook her head. "No. I couldn't sleep very well either. A sneezing attack is actually what woke me up. That mattress will be the first thing I throw out when I get this house."

"I thought we had a truce."

"Sorry. Force of habit."

"The real estate ad said everything in the house was included, right?"

Samantha nodded.

"I say we go through the stuff up here. There's got to be something worth money. I really don't think the owner knows what kind of jackpot they're sitting on with the land and house. For the life of me I can't figure out why they're selling it for so cheap."

"I know. I keep looking for the catch. It'll probably come when we sit down at the table to sign over the title," Samantha said.

Kyle stood and lifted the lid off the box where he'd been sitting. He let out a low whistle. "It's the jackpot for sure—old moth-eaten clothes."

"Just what I've always wanted," Samantha said sarcastically. She reached for a box herself and pulled the lid off. "This is interesting."

Kyle looked over her shoulder. "What is it?"

"I have no idea. Little round...thingamajigs."

Kyle reached into the box and pulled out a small cardboard tube. He pulled the cap off and his eyes lit up. "I know what these are. They're old phonograph cylinders. The earliest versions of phonographs used these cylinders instead of the round records that came later."

"How do they work?"

"The outside of the cylinder is engraved with the recording. You hook it up to the machine and it plays. My great grandma used to have one. She died when I was ten, but I remember watching her use it." Kyle set the cylinder back in the box and put his hands on his hips. "I wonder if there's a phonograph to play them on up here somewhere."

Samantha opened another box and peered into its depths. "There's not one in here, but there are more moth-eaten clothes...you know, in case you're running low."

"I'll keep that in mind if I ever decide to change my fashion style."

Samantha glanced from one stack of boxes to the next. "There's enough stuff up here to furnish the entire house."

"True, although most people these days prefer their furniture to be a little more on the modern side." Kyle grabbed the edge of a sheet thrown over an unidentified piece of furniture and pulled down. A plume of dust billowed up and he jumped back, coughing and sneezing. "That wasn't the smartest thing I've ever done," he mumbled.

Samantha quickly pulled the collar of her jacket up to cover her face. "No kidding."

"Look what's under here, though." Kyle looked over his shoulder at Samantha. "It's an old armoire."

Samantha crossed the attic floor to stand next to Kyle. "It doesn't happen to have Narnia carved into the door does it?"

Kyle grinned. "Narnia? No. But it does say 'Entrance to Neverland.'"

"Nice try."

Kyle tugged gently on the doors and they scraped open. "Nothing but dust bunnies."

"Shocker." Samantha reached for a sheet covering the furniture next to the armoire. She covered her face before pulling it off and managed to avoid sneezing. "Ooo! A vintage dining table. This would be nice to have downstairs in the kitchen right now. Do you think there're chairs to go with it somewhere?"

Kyle grabbed another furniture covering. "They're probably right here." He tugged and the sheet fell to the ground, revealing four matching dining chairs with ornate carvings in the back and upholstered cushions.

"These are in *really* good condition," Samantha said as she ran her hand along the carved back. "I think the pattern is the same as the one carved into the bed downstairs."

Kyle lifted a chair onto the table so they could examine it closer.

Samantha grabbed his arm. "Look!" She pointed to a small square carved into the back of the chair. Inside the square were the initials E.D."

"Erastus Dornea," Kyle said.

"The man had talent, that's for sure."

"It's a waste for all of this to be hidden away in the attic."

"It's sad, that's what it is."

Samantha and Kyle spent the next two hours looking through boxes and uncovering furniture. The attic contained treasures neither of them could have ever imagined. To the casual observer, the objects in the attic might be considered junk, but at least to Samantha it meant something more. Every item tucked away in that attic used to belong to someone— someone who lived and breathed and wished and dreamed and…

"You look cold," Kyle said, interrupting her thoughts. "Here, take my jacket."

The drafts in the attic were far worse than the lower floors. "No. I can't do that to you. I'll be fine." Samantha rocked back and forth on her heels.

Kyle tucked the jacket around her shoulders anyway and rubbed her arms.

"Thanks. What are *you* going to wear now?"

Kyle looked over his shoulder and nodded. "I could always wear Coleman's uniform we uncovered in his foot locker."

"Hmm…a man in uniform…" Samantha blushed, embarrassed by the words she didn't mean to say out loud.

"What are you saying?" Kyle's arms were still on hers.

"I don't know what I'm saying. The dust must be getting to me. I think I'm going to head back downstairs." She pulled his jacket off her shoulders and handed it to him before making a beeline for the staircase.

Inside the bedroom where she'd slept, she opened the curtains once more and peered out. The first rays of the morning sun were just starting to peek from between the branches of the pine trees below.

She could feel herself falling for Kyle and it scared her. He was her enemy, her nemesis, her rival, her competition. Falling for him would make fighting him too hard. It would make her weak. *I don't need a man in my life. I'm perfectly capable of surviving on my own.* She sat on the bed and drummed her fingers on the mattress. *Just because I'm capable of surviving on my own doesn't mean I have to. And Kyle seems like a good guy...* She jumped up and crossed her arms over her chest, pacing back and forth in front of the window. *What am I thinking? He probably doesn't have any feelings for me. He was just being nice up there.*

She reached for her cell phone to check the time, but the battery had died sometime during the night. "Of course," she muttered.

She plugged the lamp in one more time and dug through her black bag. "Where is my stupid charge cord? I know I packed it." Not having any success, she turned her black bag upside down on the bed—yet again—and pawed through the contents. It wasn't there. The charge cord she specifically remembered packing had disappeared. In her mind, she retraced her steps, trying to figure out at what point it fell out. She could look in the sitting room where she'd left her bag the night before, but she didn't remember the bag ever tipping over. *Could it have bounced out while Kyle and I were walking up the driveway to the house last night?*

A memory hit and she slapped herself in the forehead. "The black cat!"

"What about a black cat?" Kyle's voice came from behind.

Samantha gasped and whirled around. "You just love sneaking up on me, don't you?"

"Sorry. You left the bedroom door open so I thought it was okay." Kyle wrapped one arm around a bedpost and leaned against it. "What were you saying about a cat?"

"I'm looking for the charge cord for my phone. You haven't seen it have you?"

Kyle shook his head.

"Last night, as I was driving here, a black cat ran across the road in front of me. I slammed on my brakes and my bag fell off the seat. I'm guessing my charge cord fell out then and I didn't know. It's probably sitting on the floor of my car as we speak."

"Would you call this a desperate situation?"

Samantha eyed him suspiciously, not sure what he was getting at. "Well...my phone's dead. I need it to stay up on my business while I'm here and, at the very least, I'll need it to call Mr. Hargrave when you give up and need the gate unlocked."

"How much would it be worth to you?"

Samantha sat up straighter. "Do you know where it is? Did I drop it in the house somewhere?"

"No, but I brought a cord. You're welcome to borrow it."

"What's the catch?"

Kyle waved a hand at the pile of stuff strewn across the bed. "Share some of your sustenance and the cord is all yours."

Samantha raised her eyebrows. "Don't tell me you didn't pack any food."

"I brought a bag of beef jerky. It's not exactly the breakfast of champions." A grin spread across his face. "Honestly? If I'd had any inkling that *you* would be the other party, I would have prepared better. When I agreed to do this, I thought I'd be out of here within a couple of hours."

Samantha hesitated. A starving Kyle might end the game sooner, but she really needed her phone. "Help yourself," she finally said.

"Thanks." Kyle reached down and chose one of the energy bars. "I plugged my phone into the outlet in the sitting room last night. I'm sure it's fully charged by now so you're welcome to use it."

"You don't happen to know the time do you?"

Kyle pushed up the sleeve of his jacket and looked at his watch. "It's just after eight."

"By any chance, do you feel like leaving?"

"Not even close."

Samantha smiled. "I had to check."

Downstairs, Kyle unplugged his phone and offered the cord to Samantha. "Have at it. I'm going to go make some calls."

Alone again, Samantha wandered into the music room. She wished she knew how to play the piano like Kyle. It would be a good way to pass the time, especially since they'd uncovered boxes of music in the attic. The pages had yellowed with age, but the notes were still legible. She walked to the wall of bookshelves and began straightening the few remaining books. She blew off the dust and read the title of each book in turn. Almost all were classics, but there were a few she'd never heard of before.

The most surprising find came a few minutes after she started. Tucked on a bottom shelf, a brown-leather covered book with no writing on the cover lay forgotten. Samantha picked it up and opened the front cover. Her breath caught in her throat when she read the words written by hand in faded black ink. '*Dornea Pines—A History*' written by Diana Dornea.

Chapter *11*

O h wow…" Samantha whispered as she rubbed her fingers across the brittle pages of the book. "This is amazing. Diana wrote it all by hand."

Samantha carried the book across the hall and sat down on the settee, kicking off her shoes and tucking her legs beneath her. She began to read.

Diana's flowery handwriting made it hard to decipher some of the words, but Samantha couldn't put the book down. Diana wrote about the building of Dornea Pines and how happy she was the day they were finally able to move in. She wrote about carefully picking each piece of furniture, many of which Samantha recognized as pieces tucked away in the attic.

Diana wrote of happy times and sad times. She wrote of the births of grandchildren and the deaths of dear friends. She wrote of political happenings and local events. The pages were filled with observations and deep descriptions.

And then she wrote of the death of her beloved Erastus.

Even if Samantha didn't already know that Erastus' death was a turning point for Diana, she would have known something changed as soon as she read the pages of history after his death.

Diana's writing changed. The letters slanted more and the overall words became sloppier, as if Diana suddenly sped up her writing pace, needing to get everything on the page quickly.

The words on the pages were haunting. Diana believed her house was possessed by some entity that wouldn't let her leave her room. She wrote of fears and paranoia that would have terrified Samantha if she weren't reading in the light of day. The times when Coleman came to visit, Diana's writing returned to its original clean appearance and nothing was mentioned of anything evil.

The date on the last handwritten page fell on June 18, 1918. "*A telegram arrived today at exactly 11:00 a.m. I heard the clock in the downstairs hall chime just before the knock came on the front door. My maid, Sariah, brought the telegram to my room and I knew the moment I saw it what it would say. I didn't want to read it, but I knew I must. My worst fears were confirmed. Coleman is gone. I will never see my sweet and caring son again. His life was cut short in a Great War he didn't start and didn't need to be fighting. He is my rock. I fear I cannot go on living without him.*"

Tears slid down Samantha's cheeks as she read Diana's final entry.

"Sam? Are you okay?"

Samantha jumped at the sound of Kyle's voice. Embarrassed, she turned away and wiped at the tears sliding down her face with the back of her hand before responding. "Sorry. I'm just...I...umm..."

"That must be some book you're reading." Kyle pointed toward her lap.

"It's a history of Dornea Pines. Diana wrote it."

"Where'd you get it?"

"I found it on one of the shelves in the music room."

Kyle sat down next to her and her heart fluttered. His fingers brushed hers as she transferred the book to his hands and she silently chastised herself for noticing.

"This is cool." He gently turned each page, not taking time to read them, but looking in awe at the lines of faded ink. "I wonder if the owner knows it's here."

"I doubt it. It was covered in dust and didn't look as if it has been opened in decades. Kyle, I think Diana went crazy. After Erastus died, she wrote weird ramblings about the house being possessed. The only times her writings were normal was when Coleman was around. Do you think she went insane?"

"Maybe. It's possible."

"It's sad. Before Erastus died, Dornea Pines was filled with life and happiness. It was a gathering place for the community and their family welcomed everyone with open arms. Diana wrote that Erastus was considering a run for the mayor's office, but he got sick and passed away before he got the chance. Read the final entry."

Kyle turned to the last written page and silently read. Samantha watched him, enjoying the way his lips formed each word as his fingers traced over the page. "Coleman's death and Diana's last straw." He eased the book back into Samantha's hands. His fingers brushed against hers again and he let them linger, meeting her eyes and smiling before pulling his hand away.

He's doing it on purpose. He's flirting with me! Samantha closed the book, but a small piece of paper drifted out, floating down to rest on her lap.

"What's that?" Kyle asked.

"I'm not sure." She picked up the note and read it aloud. "Diana Dornea was found dead in her room two days after her last entry. That's all it says. It's not signed."

"You don't think she ended her own life, do you?" Kyle asked.

"I'm not sure what to think. All I know is that these walls contain more history than all the homes I've previously flipped put together." She chewed on her lower lip as she drummed her fingers on the leather cover of Diana's history. Something had been nagging at Samantha ever since she and Kyle went through the furnishings in the attic during the night.

"Something wrong?" Kyle asked.

"No...I mean, yes. It's just that...I'm starting to have second thoughts about this place."

Kyle rested his arm on the back of the settee and raised his eyebrows. "Really? You don't want it anymore?"

Samantha shook her head back and forth, her ponytail flapping. "No. That's not it at all. She set the book on the cushion next to her and stood up. "If anything, I want Dornea Pines even more than when we arrived last night. But...I don't want to tear it down and completely change it just to flip it for a little profit."

"What are you saying? Do you want to live here?"

"No. That's not it either." Samantha clasped her hands together. She couldn't believe what she was about to say. "I want to buy it and fix it up and turn it into a museum or something. So much of that stuff up in the attic is part of this town's history. Everything has been well preserved. It doesn't make sense to just get rid of it. School groups could come through, families could visit... It's probably a stupid idea, but I seriously don't feel like this place should be changed."

Kyle stood and stuffed his hands in his pockets. "I think we might have been having the same thoughts. There aren't many old homes with this much acreage left. All morning I've been thinking that this place would make a great event location."

"What do you mean?"

"Did you know there's a gazebo outside?"

Samantha shook her head.

"It's in the trees in the backyard. I wandered around out there while making phone calls just now. Some of the rails are rotting and the roof will need new shingles, but it's in a great spot to see the valley and the lake. It would make a great spot for a wedding ceremony." Kyle crossed to where Samantha paced in front of the window and put a hand on her shoulder. "There's a barn out there, too," he said excitedly. "It's really old and will probably need to be completely torn down and rebuilt, but it could easily be a venue for a reception."

Samantha nodded along with him. "Or a family reunion... Instead of putting fancy tables and linens in there, we could fill it with picnic tables to keep the casual feel. There will be plenty of room for parking if we tear out a few trees. Not the pine trees, of course, but some of the scrubby ones in an inconspicuous area. The original acreage will be preserved and—"

She stopped talking when Kyle reached out and took her hands in his. "We?" he said.

Confused, she narrowed her eyes at him.

"You said we. *We* will fill it with picnic tables. *We* tear out the trees for parking."

"I meant my crew."

Kyle shook his head. "Let's do it together. We've both become attached to this place and we both have the same reservations about flipping it. If the house itself is returned to its original state to host tours and we rent out the rest of the property for events, we'll make money. You and I can do this together."

Samantha's heart pounded in her chest. Working with Kyle had never crossed her mind, but she'd completely changed her opinion of him since they arrived the night before. Many of their wishes and desires were the same. "Let's do it." The words fell out of her mouth of their own free will.

Kyle grinned. "Really?"

"Really." She laughed.

Kyle let out a whoop and swooped her up in his arms, spinning around in a circle before setting her back down. "This is going to be amazing. I can't wait to get started. We'll do as much research as possible before we demo anything, of course. I'm sure the library will have books that have information about the Dornea family."

"And we'll fix up the cemetery section. It could be part of the tour of the house."

Kyle rubbed his fingers along the back of her palms. "We should probably fix the organ. Wouldn't want anyone else thinking this place is haunted."

Samantha punched him in the arm playfully. "Ha ha. Very funny. Actually, I think including the ghost stories would be an important part of the tour. The stories are part of the home's history, too. Maybe we could do a special Halloween version of the tour. If the home is alive and active on the holiday, it will prevent teens from doing any damage."

"I like the way you think." He let go of her hands and then stuck his right hand out toward her. "Do we have a deal?"

She took his hand and shook it. "We have a deal."

"Can we call Mr. Hargrave then? I really need a shower."

Samantha laughed. "I'll make the call." She unplugged her phone from Kyle's charge cord and dialed Mr. Hargrave's number.

He answered on the second ring. "Ms. Alwood, I'm surprised to hear from you," he said upon answering. "I must admit I fully expected Mr. Shipton to be the one throwing in the towel first."

"I'm not calling to quit. I'm calling to tell you we've come to a compromise. Mr. Shipton and I want to purchase the property together. We plan to preserve Dornea Pines."

Mr. Hargrave remained silent on the other end of the line for a long moment. "You have both agreed to this?"

"We have. If it's okay with the owner, we'll get our financing in order and go ahead with the deal as soon as possible."

"I'll need to make a phone call, of course, but I'm sure it won't be a problem." He cleared his throat. "I assume this means you want me to come unlock the gate?"

Samantha smiled to herself. "That would be *much* appreciated."

"What'd he say?" Kyle asked when she turned off her phone.

"He doesn't think it will be a problem. He's on his way to let us out."

"I haven't felt this excited about anything in a long time."

"I know what you mean. I feel alive."

"Of course, some of that could be due to the girl I've been privileged to spend the night with...and the prospect of spending more time with that same girl."

Samantha felt a hint of red popping out on her cheeks. "Oh? Spending time with this girl makes you happy?"

"Very much."

"I think it makes the girl happy, too."

Kyle reached up and gently touched her face. She leaned into his palm. His lips met hers at the same time his other hand slipped around her waist.

Samantha melted into his kiss and embrace, no longer fighting her feelings.

"This is just one of the perks of making a deal with me," Kyle said with a grin. "Give me an hour to go home and get cleaned up and I'll take you out for a proper date—I mean, business lunch."

"Sounds good to me," she whispered into his hair. "I think I'm going to like working with you."

ABOUT THE AUTHOR

Author Tifani Clark grew up on a farm in southeastern Idaho (yes, that's where they grow all the potatoes) as the middle of five children. She had a lot of space to imagine and daydream and often pictured herself as a character in one of the many books she read. She was habitually found pretending to be Scarlett O'Hara. She is married to the love of her life and is the mother to four fabulous children. When not writing, she enjoys playing the violin and piano and traveling to new places. She especially enjoys visits to national parks and places of historical significance.

IF YOU ENJOYED ONE NIGHT AT DORNEA PINES, GO ONLINE AND LEAVE A REVIEW. THANKS!

www.ingramcontent.com/pod-product-compliance
Lightning Source LLC
Chambersburg PA
CBHW071324130626
46556CB00004B/1739